DEFENDERS OF TIME | BOOK 2

KIDNAPPERS FROM THE FUTURE

INDIGORIVER
PUBLISHING

DEFENDERS OF TIME | BOOK 2

KIDNAPPERS FROM THE FUTURE

GENE P. ABEL

The sequel to *GOING BACK*

Indigo River Publishing
3 West Garden Street, Ste. 718
Pensacola, FL 32502
www.indigoriverpublishing.com

Kidnappers from the Future | Gene P. Abel, author
ISBN: 978-1-950906-92-5 (paperback)
LCCN: 2020925769

Edited by Earl Tillinghast
Cover and interior design by Robin Vuchnich

Special discounts are available on quantity purchases by corporations, associations, and others. For details, contact the publisher at the address above.

Orders by US trade bookstores and wholesalers: Please contact the publisher at the address above.

My continuing thanks to my wonderful wife, Susan Anne, for her help and never-ending encouragement. I also want to thank Morry for his help with the publication process, and the staff at Indigo River Publishing.

I

INCIDENT AT LOS ALAMOS

Los Alamos, New Mexico, is the home of the most famous lab in the world, a place where quiet suburban life exists alongside cutting-edge scientific research in a small foothill community. It is a collection of small colleges, lazy downtown life, and a merciless noontime sun. During World War II, when they housed the historic Manhattan Project, each of the labs contained classified research while their educated populace enjoyed the quiet small-town life.

Known only to a select few was also the city's relative proximity to a facility even more secretive than the Manhattan Project. A government facility located some odd miles away in the middle of the desert that to outside eyes may have appeared as a few dusty old buildings. But beneath that exterior lay a small city under military supervision that was home to Project Enlightenment, where time travel had been made a reality. Mankind's greatest scientific achievement, as well as his greatest responsibility.

For a brief time, however, such things would not concern two members of that project.

Dr. Sam Weiss and Special Agent Lou Hessman were walking slowly down the middle of a large quadrangle, before them a massive convention hall with walls of gleaming steel and polished glass, its two-story foyer busy with the gathering crowd entering in through its line of clear glass doors. All around the square other people meandered slowly between one building and another of those bordering it. It was a Friday and the clock tower that loomed over the northeast section of the square was just striking 11:00 a.m. as they continued to walk, with Sam bearing two things about his person: a broad smile and a walking cane.

"Honestly, Lou, I don't need a nursemaid," Dr. Weiss amiably objected. "I've been on my feet for a couple months now."

"You're a key scientist for the project," Agent Hessman replied, "and still under recovery, or you wouldn't need that cane."

"Actually I'm thinking of keeping the cane even after I'm fully recovered," Dr. Weiss said. "Makes me look rather stylish, don't you think?"

Even as they talked, Agent Hessman's eyes never left their duty of darting rapidly through the crowd surging lazily past, assessing every face for a possible threat. It didn't matter if they looked like an absent-minded intellect or a talkative pair of college students, he took them all in.

"There's another reason why I had to get out of the lab," Dr. Weiss said after a couple more steps.

"Phelps," Hessman replied with a nod.

"The poor boy in a coma all this time, then . . . I wish he could have pulled through."

"At least the general gave him a nice service. As far as his family will know, Lieutenant David Phelps died in service to his country."

"They just will never know what that really meant." Dr. Weiss sighed. "Or what he meant to our team . . . Harris—how is she doing?"

"Still in a coma last I checked," Agent Hessman replied. "She's a fighter, but her doctors have no idea when or if she'll pull through."

Dr. Weiss replied with silence, focusing on the quad they were walking across and the people passing by with smiles and eager talk. It was a full minute before Agent Hessman snapped them both out of their sorrowful reverie with a question.

"So, this niece of yours we're supposed to meet," he prompted.

"Samantha, my brother's child. Yes, I think you'll like her. She was just finishing up her PhD when we had the first unfortunate conference."

"And now she's attending Time Conference two point oh? That's another reason why I'm here. If—or *when*—some terrorist strikes this one, I want to be ready."

"Lou, surely lightning will not strike twice. It's been three months since that happened. I'm sure things will be entirely peaceful."

"And *that*," Agent Hessman emphasized, "is yet another reason why I'm here with you. Your naïveté."

"And *that*," Dr. Weiss said, pointing off into the crowd with his cane, "is my niece."

Agent Hessman glanced up to see the one Dr. Weiss indicated. Just from mention of her doctorate, he'd expected much the stereotypical image of a female lab rat with her hair done up in a bun and square glasses fixed on her nose. What he saw, however, caught him completely off guard.

She walked with a natural poise and grace, bearing a smile that seemed as honest and natural to her as breathing. Long brunette locks spilled out over her shoulders in lazy curls, with no prim glasses to camouflage the beauty of her features or the energetic gleam in her eyes. In place of the anticipated lab coat she wore a long white and pastel blue summer dress that draped just past her knees. In short, she was a statuesque beauty.

When she saw Dr. Weiss her smile broadened and she waved eagerly before quickening her pace to close the distance between them. "Uncle Sam!" she exclaimed, beaming. She took him in a full hug, then released him for a quick appraising look. "You have a cane. Did you injure yourself? What happened?"

"Only the occasional dizzy spell to be cautious of," Dr. Weiss replied. "It happened three months ago as a result of . . . a certain project that you're here to join."

"Oh yes," she said with a knowing nod. "I read the mission report. You know, I may have a few ideas that can help with the accuracy of the scanners. If we just increase the field density of the emission coil, then we can—"

The nature of the pending discussion snapped Agent Hessman out of his stunned reverie and immediately back to his job.

"If you don't mind," he quickly interjected, "could you save the temporal shoptalk for far more secure conditions?"

Dr. Weiss chuckled, and said, "Oh, I'm sorry. Leave us to our common interests and we'll be at this for hours. Sam, this is my protector and friend, Special Agent Lou Hessman. He's in charge of security back at the facility. Lou, this is my niece, Samantha Weiss. Doctorate in physics, specializing in the theory of time travel and its consequences, and as brilliant as she is lovely."

Samantha smiled as she offered a hand. "Lou, how very nice to meet you."

They both paused as their hands touched, each seeing within the other something special; for Lou that meant a stunning beauty framing the promise of a sharp mind. Though in truth it was only a moment's pause, not even long enough for Dr. Weiss to notice, to Agent Hessman it seemed like an hour.

"Nice to meet you, Miss . . ."

"Just call me Samantha," she replied, easing from her own momentary pause of uncertainty back into a ready smile. "Or Sam."

"Sam? Wait," Agent Hessman said as he came to the realization. "But that's . . ."

"I was named after my uncle. Either that or a character on an old sitcom, depending on who you ask."

Agent Hessman couldn't help but grin at the reference, which was an act that *did* get Dr. Weiss's attention. The smile was brief, but it was there and stood out for the fact that Dr. Weiss had never seen the government agent so much as twitch his upper lip. He said nothing of it, though, just mused to himself before cutting into the conversation.

"Samantha is not what most people would expect of a PhD, and she can talk as readily about how to bait a hook as physics."

"Something which *you* taught me to do when you came with me and Dad on those fishing trips when I was a kid."

"You fish?" Agent Hessman asked.

"No one really fishes on those kinds of trips," Samantha replied. "It's really just an excuse for talking shop, which in my dad's case meant talking chemistry while Uncle Sam talked physics, and me in the middle."

"I would be forever annoying your father," Dr. Weiss said with a chuckle, "by pointing out that chemistry is a subcategory of physics."

"Which it technically is," Samantha said with a slight giggle herself, "but that didn't stop Dad from pouting for half the trip, trying to think up a counterargument. But about the cane: How long are you going to be needing it?"

"Oh, don't worry about that, Sam. I almost don't need it right now, but I'm thinking of keeping it as a stylish affectation. Think it might get me some more respect when I walk into the conference with this?"

"You are the most respected scientists I know, Uncle. Oh, but aren't we going to be late for the panel?"

"Sam and I are registered to attend a panel at eleven thirty," Dr. Weiss said for Agent Hessman's benefit, "but it's been so long since I've seen my lovely niece that I think we should skip the first panel and go to lunch. My treat. We have a lot to catch up on."

"Skip the conference?" Samantha asked.

"Just the one panel. We can be back in time for the next one at three. There are a number of lovely little eateries a short way from here that I'm sure Lou's security sensibilities would approve of."

"Well, I guess it *has* been a while," she agreed. Then, with an eye for Agent Hessman: "What do you think, Lou? Any particular place that you'd recommend?"

For the second time Agent Hessman was brought up short by those perfect eyes being aimed in his direction, but this time he recovered more quickly with an answer that sounded all professional—on the surface, at least.

"There is a little sandwich shop with a back patio secure from direct line of sight from any neighboring buildings, and nothing but an open view of the mesa. It should be secure enough."

"It sounds perfect," she said. "Lunch with a view. And good company."

"You and your uncle should have plenty of privacy to chat."

"I'm sure we will, Lou. Why don't you take the lead and show us the way."

"I would be glad to," Agent Hessman replied with a courteous nod.

"And I'll act as chaperone," Dr. Weiss muttered under his breath with a very slight grin.

"That is," Agent Hessman continued, "it is my duty to see to your safety as well now since you'll be joining the project."

"Either way," Samantha said, slipping her right arm into Agent Hessman's left, "I will have two perfect gentlemen to escort me."

She then slipped her left arm into the crook of Dr. Weiss's right, putting herself in the middle. It seemed to Dr. Weiss that Lou looked a little uncomfortable at that moment, but he said nothing, only grinned to himself as his niece turned her attention more to his protector than himself.

They would not get very far, however. The peaceful small-town atmosphere was interrupted by a commotion coming from the large conference building ahead of them. People shouting, the sound of gunfire, and through the large glass windows that comprised the front wall of the building's expansive foyer they could see men in black uniforms with the word security printed across their chests and backs brandishing their guns in a chase through the crowd of suddenly screaming conference attendees.

While Samantha and Dr. Weiss looked on curiously, Agent Hessman went immediately into action. Releasing himself from Samantha, he whipped out a pistol just as three men burst through the screaming crowd and out the front entry for a quick look across the open quad, giving the people sudden cause to scatter.

"Down!" Agent Hessman ordered his two charges.

One of the three strangers guarded their backs, sending off a shot at the nearest approaching security guard. It didn't sound like any normal shot, however; more like an electrical snap and a high-speed hiss accompanied by a flash of light at the mouth of the pistol's barrel. The bullet slammed into the chest of the first guard with a bright flash of light that shoved him off his feet and into the next guard behind him.

Dr. Weiss and Samantha

Meanwhile, the other two had maintained their position, their quick scan of the crowd ending with a direct look in the direction of Agent Hessman and his two charges. One of the men spoke to the other in quick syllables, but not in anything resembling English.

"That sounds like Russian," Samantha remarked as she and her uncle hit the ground.

The three men had dark features and nondescript jumpsuits, but very distinctive pistols. They wasted no time and started swiftly for the group of three, one of them raising his pistol as its barrel began sparking electrically.

"Hold it right there," Agent Hessman called out.

Hessman was crouched down on one knee, both hands on his pistol, taking aim. Behind him Samantha and Dr. Weiss crouched low, while from another building across the quad, more men in security uniforms were running over to join the disturbance.

"One more step," Agent Hessman called out to them, "and the first one's dead!"

Hessman didn't wait for that step. He saw the middle man's finger on the trigger starting to pull back, and fired. He aimed straight for the man's head, yet his bullet was slightly off. In the flash of the moment his bullet caught the man's gun hand just off to the side, spoiling his aim just enough so that the next shot that came out of the strange pistol whizzed by Agent Hessman's ear and instead slammed into a post somewhere behind him with a bright spark of light.

In the next moment, a small army of security personnel came across the quad to join them, filling in behind the three gunmen as well as alongside Agent Hessman. A few words between the three in what sounded like more Russian and they broke off, turning away to head for the side of the nearest building. A second shot from Agent Hessman began a hail of gunfire from the army of security personnel, which chewed up the concrete behind the men as they ducked around the corner, with Hessman breaking into a run after them.

"Secure the quad," Hessman shouted as he ran, "and get those gunmen!"

Agent Hessman himself was first to round the corner not more than a couple of seconds behind them, alongside him several of the security personnel. He expected to see his quarry still trying to make good their escape, but what he found was . . . nothing. No flapping door to give away an escape route, no overturned garbage can, not so much as a leaf stirred.

To the confused look of the first guard to his side he gave an order: "Search the whole area."

"Yes, sir."

As security personnel scurried to cordon off the area, Samantha came up with her uncle limping along by her side.

"It appears that I still have some need for this cane," Dr. Weiss remarked as they approached. "At least when getting up from an unexpected kneeling position."

"They sounded Russian," Samantha said. "And those guns of theirs. Lou, who were they?"

"A very good question," Agent Hessman answered. His gaze, as he talked, was fixed on the ground ahead of him, studying it.

"Well, I guess lightning really does strike twice," Dr. Weiss remarked. "A good thing they increased security the way you told them to. But what would some Russians be doing around here? What do they want? And how'd they even get in?"

"I have some even better questions," Agent Hessman absently replied, his gaze still fixed on the ground. "Like, why is there not so much as a single drop of blood around here? As many bullets as were flying out, I'd think at least a few of them would have hit them. Even accounting for body armor . . . but nothing. And now they vanish?"

"I think you have a point," Dr. Weiss agreed. "But what does it mean?"

"It means," Agent Hessman said, with a last look down at the empty ground before facing his two companions, "that the conference is on hold. Again. I'm taking the two of you directly back to base. Samantha, you're headed there anyway; now it's just a bit sooner than expected. I'll have your things sent over, but neither of you is leaving my sight until you're secure."

"Understood," she replied, all business now. "Any suspicions?"

One of the security guards came up to them, holding up a clear baggy with some sort of expended bullet casing in it. The design, though, was very unusual.

"From whatever it was they fired, sir," the security man explained as he handed it off. "Sir, if this is a shell casing, I've never seen anything like it before."

To Agent Hessman's nod, the man left to go to other duties, leaving him with a puzzle in his hand.

"I may have a few," Agent Hessman then replied to Samantha. "And I think it's time to recall Ben and Claire."

"That's right," Dr. Weiss remarked. "He's been showing her around some of the sights of the modern world. No telling where they are right now, though."

"I've been keeping track," Agent Hessman blandly replied, "as is my duty. Right now, they should be in New York City."

2

FIRST DATE

"This is the only way to see New York."

Professor Ben Stein was dressed in his preferred baggy clothes with many pockets, but had at least cleaned himself up a bit for the company he was keeping. With his short black hair slicked back and a clean shave, he was holding hands with the one beside him, Claire Hill, lately of the very early twentieth century, now with an updated wardrobe, although she had kept her wide-brimmed, floppy white hat that was the style back in the year 1919. Gone, though, were the boots, replaced with a stylish pair of Teva "Verra" sandals. Her dress was more pastel in coloration and less the highly layered look, though it still reached down to her ankles. At five and a half feet tall and slender, with long black hair, a pearly white complexion, and blue eyes, she was a beauty in any century.

They were on the observation deck of the Freedom Tower, with its wraparound glass-walled lounge, intimidating Sky Portal view to the hundred-story drop below, and the eager crowd taking in the awe-inspiring view around them. Ben and Claire spoke quietly to be certain no one could overhear their conversation.

For Claire it was something more approaching terrifying as she took in the view with a belch, and a death grip on Ben's left hand with her right.

"Sorry about that. That hotdog was great, but it's coming back up on me a little."

Ben grinned. "Sabrett's will do that to you."

She looked once again to the view: the horizon of skyscrapers, the immense bridges that now seemed so small from this angle, the rivers and the distant ocean and the massive vessels plying them, and any number of inspiring details that Ben could only imagine were catching her attention.

"I can't believe this view. Those buildings all looked so tall from the ground, but now they're so far down. Any higher and I swear we'd touch heaven. You can see the entire island, across the river, the harbor, all the way to the ocean. I think you can even see the curvature of the earth from here! And look, another plane. There must be more of those things than birds. I never could have imagined anything like what I'm seeing now."

"It's an unbelievable view, even for those of us more local to the time period," Ben agreed.

"Well, I think I'm going to faint. You sure this glass wall is strong enough? Oh, and look at those ships down there! Back in my time the docks were crowded with steamships and a few with sails; now there's a lot less of them, but they're so *huge*. We had so many belching out all that smoke, you could barely see through it around the docks at times, but now you got these things that look like floating skyscrapers lying on their sides. Oh, and all those bridges. I had the Brooklyn Bridge, but what are all those others?"

"Well," Ben said, pointing out each one in turn, "that's the Washington Bridge; then over that way is the Manhattan Bridge. There are some pretty historic buildings as well. That one over there? That's the Empire State Building, built back in the thirties. It's sort of the city mascot."

"After my time," Claire said with a grin. "We had the Woolworth Building and thought that was pretty amazing."

"It still is; the lobby's open for tours even now. Then there's the Chrysler Building, and . . . well, so many others. Just take your time absorbing it all. I'll take you to anything that hits your fancy. I just want to see you happy."

"I think that's far too soft a word for what I'm feeling right now. All the things you've shown me . . . Even after a couple months of touring around them movies, I just can't believe those things□ —the sound, the pictures, and the size of that *screen*! I still don't get half the references they make, but it makes going to a play look pretty tame. Oh, and that museum we saw!"

"The Met," Ben replied. "I don't know how long it's been there, but I imagine the collections have become much larger since your time."

"Around 1870, if I recall. That place is even older than *me*." She added a giggle when she said this, then tossed a smile to Ben. "I still get the giggles when I say things like that. I'm the oldest person on the planet right now and not a day over twenty-four."

For a moment when she said that, her smile froze uncertainly on her face, her gaze distant.

"Sorry about that," she said after a moment, "but every so often it hits me. All my old friends, my family, they're all dead and gone; I'll never see them again."

"You have some new friends," Ben said with a soft smile. "We'll help you through it."

Some of her comments got an odd look from one passerby or another, but she simply ignored them as she took in the expansive New York skyline while her right hand reflexively slipped from Ben's grip and snaked itself around his waist. For a moment they just stood there like that, Ben enjoying the company far more than the sights but unsure how to proceed. The moment finally ended rather suddenly with a kiss from Claire directly on his lips.

"What was that for? Not that I mind, of course."

"For saving my life. And for being here right now. I would have died of influenza a century back if not for your time's medical miracles. Of all the things that I've seen, from televisions to those little ovens that cook things in a minute or two, I think the fact that you've wiped the likes of smallpox from the face of the planet is the most amazing. I can only imagine how much better things are going to get in the next century."

"Well, stick around," he said with a grin. "Maybe you'll find a way to see *that* century as well."

"Only with you by my side. You're my anchor in this new world you've brought me to."

Ben could feel himself blushing, and he knew that Claire could see it, but it only endeared him to her all the more. Then her glance fell to some of the other tourists walking across the observation lounge, specifically one young lady in a pair of new jeans that looked as if they had been purposefully shredded from hip to heel, Nike sneakers, and a baggy T-shirt with a nearly obscene graphic design, and with a large amount of very loud makeup on her face.

"I can't say much for the modern fashion sense, though," Claire remarked. "I think there are still a few things that your century can learn from mine."

"It's your century too now, remember." Then, as Ben glanced over to the one she was looking at, he added, "Though I see your point. It looks like she really shoveled on that makeup."

"Ben, if you're going to insult something, then you need a writer's touch. Something to leave the other wondering if they've been insulted or not until you're safely out of sight."

"Okay then, Miss Hill," he said, grinning, "go to it. Let's see what you've got."

"Challenge accepted."

Claire stood there for a few seconds thinking, her gaze never leaving the other young woman, until she came up with her insult, though for Ben's ears alone.

"Her makeup looks like a perfect sunset was trapped in one of your microwave ovens for too long, while her clothes look like the result of an unfortunate accident involving a wheat combine while trying to save a lost puppy, though it's just a shame that said puppy got smeared all over her shirt like that. I can understand the shoes, though; I'd want to be ready to run, too, if I dressed like that."

Ben couldn't help it: his growing smirk exploded into outright laughter of such intensity that he had to turn away from view of the passing young woman and face the New York skyline again. When the young woman glanced over to see what someone found so funny, Claire just smiled, gave a slight curtsey with one partially bent knee, then turned back to Ben and the view of the city.

"But that's just off the top of my head, mind you," she said to him.

Once he had contained himself, Ben reached down and planted a quick kiss on her lips.

"Now what was *that* for?"

"Being the perfect lady," he replied. "At least for me."

"Well then, that's something else you can learn from my time, because as far as a kiss from a man to his girl goes, that was pretty lackluster."

"Insults now? You realize we're having a moment here."

"All the more reason to get it right."

"Oh, you mean like in those really old movies I showed you?"

"First, keep in mind that those old movies are still *after* my time—and you're going to have to show me more of them so I know what the heck you're talking about□ —and second, yes. Here, I'll get you started."

So saying, she pulled his arms around her waist, reached up to tilt his head down, then wrapped her arms around his back and drew herself in close.

"Oh," he said, "you mean more like this?"

His lips touched hers, lightly at first, then pressing all the more as he drew her nearer. It was as if a snap of energy had suddenly gone off between them, holding them there together. His hands squeezed her shoulders lightly, while her bosom pressed into his chest. It was infinity in a moment for them both, a new energy arising within each that wanted release. The moment come to its apex with the last crowning touch as Claire bent her right knee and gave the classic pose.

When they finally broke for air Claire's face was spotted with sweat, her breath a quick pant as she swallowed before replying. "Yeah, like that."

Ben smiled. "I'm a quick study."

It was their perfect moment, and like most perfect moments, it was short-lived. They both noticed that several of the passing tourists were aiming their cell phones in their direction. To Claire's questioning look, Ben could only shrug as one woman remarked eagerly to her companions and whomever else might be listening in on her phone, "I'm hashtagging this 'Perfect Kiss.' It'll be trending within the hour."

"Sorry, Claire," Ben said. "I've explained about social media."

"Not one of your century's better innovations, I have to say. Though from a reporter's point of view I can see the benefits. Say, before we start trending, how's about we start walking? I'm sure there's other places you can show me."

She said this with a smile, which Ben completely missed the meaning of.

"Plenty," he began. "We haven't been to Coney Island yet, and then there's—"

"Not what I had in mind," she said, looking directly into his eyes. "I know you're trying to be careful of my century-old sensibilities, but don't you think it's been long enough?"

"Oh. You mean . . ."

Her grin grew even more suggestive, her eyes twinkling.

One minute later where they had stood was empty of their presence, the elevator that now carried them not going down fast enough for their tastes.

* * *

In time they had another view of the New York skyline: that from a hotel room in one of the finer places that New York City had to offer. In fact, for a couple of hours they saw nothing outside of that room, just each other, and that view was quite intimate indeed. Amid all the wonders and splendors of the modern age that Claire was still able to marvel over, there was only one marvel that she cared for above all, and only one wondrous sight that would forever after catch Ben's attention.

Sunset was just coming through the window when they took a pause from their passionate encounter. The light filtering through the thin curtain drawn across the window outlined Claire's naked form in a glowing aura that made of her an angel from Ben's view. He lay there on the bed taking it in as Claire looked out across the city.

"It's still a magnificent view," she remarked.

When he said nothing, she called back over her shoulder, "Isn't this where you're supposed to make some innuendo about how it certainly is, when you really mean me?"

"I was thinking of that, but that line is just so overused. Do you know how many movies use some knockoff of that same line?"

"Well, I haven't seen hardly any of them, so it's still new to me. The advantages of being a century out-of-date: you can try all your old lines on me and they'll still work."

Her attention was fixed on the view outside and all the little wonders she might never get used to. From the sight of the many cars flooding the streets to the distant lights of Times Square starting in with their evening glow to even a jet racing by across the sky above, all of it held new wonder for her.

"Of all the places you've taken me—the cities, those spectacular amusement parks, that big cruise liner—and all the modern wonders that you've shown me, there is still nothing to compare to a perfect sunset. Especially from twenty stories up in the air."

She took in a deep breath and slowly released it as she watched the sun cast its golden rays over the tops of the city's skyscrapers.

"It's one of the few things that hasn't changed since my time. My time: I say it like it was so long ago, but for me it was just a few months. There is nothing about this world that I know anymore, no one around that knows my face. My parents, friends, that old deli I used to go to—all of it completely gone, changed beyond belief. Except for that sunset, that's still the one thing I can call my own."

She sighed and continued to watch the sun drop below the horizon, for a moment lost within herself.

"No matter how many centuries I may see, there are some things that will never grow out of fashion."

When she heard nothing in reply, she turned around to see what was wrong, then immediately cast her eyes down. Ben was down before her on one knee, in his hand a single small ring in its open felt-lined box.

"I quite agree," he softly replied.

Claire gasped in shock, hands going to her mouth as Ben looked up into her eyes. "Oh my gosh!"

"And the fact that you think that 'gosh' is not a quaint, outdated term endears you to me the more. Claire Hill, would you do me the extreme honor of—"

"Yes!"

She held out a shaking left hand, her face quickly flexing through various expressions of joy and nervousness. Ben managed to hold himself steady enough to take the ring out and gently slip it on her finger. Then he rose to his feet to greet her with a kiss. He was barely all the way up, though, when Claire beat him to it.

She flung her arms around his neck, boosted herself up for a full kiss, and wrapped her legs around his hips. One kiss came after another, barely giving Ben time for breath or to properly get his footing. He was assailed by a series of *I love yous* muttered between rapid lip-locking assaults, all while he reached under her legs to hold her up as he stepped back to balance himself. When his foot unexpectedly hit the edge of the bed he went tumbling back to land on the mattress.

Claire didn't even pause in her loving assault.

"I'm going to . . . make love to you . . . all night, until—"

Her barrage was abruptly cut off by an unexpected rendition of "Secret Agent Man" erupting from on top of the bed's nightstand. A sharp scream and she was sitting bolt upright, quickly looking around while trying to cover her breasts with her hands. When she saw no one in the room but Ben, her gaze narrowed to the nightstand.

"Just my cell phone," he said with a chuckle.

"I am *still* not used to that thing. I thought a band had snuck in here or something. Any way that you can just turn that thing off? Or maybe chuck it out the window so I can get back to ravaging you."

"Chuck?"

Claire shrugged. "I've been trying to catch up on euphemisms."

"Well, that particular ringtone means that it's Agent Hessman, which probably means that—"

She sighed. "I'll get dressed, then start packing. You see what he wants."

While Claire got off him to go gather her things, Ben pulled himself over to the nightstand and his phone, where a text message was waiting for him. It was a simple line that spoke volumes for their immediate future.

Vacation over; we had an incident.

3

TOURS AND UPGRADES

"I must say, it looks good on you, Miss Hill."

Although Claire had on a new pastel-colored knee-length summer dress and silver sandals, and her long hair was resting on her shoulders, Dr. Weiss was not referring to any of that, but to the one accoutrement that counts for a young lady with a certain kind of smile on her face: the new ring on her finger. She was walking alongside Ben as Dr. Weiss led them down a long white corridor of the base hidden beneath the New Mexico desert, the base that was the home of Project Enlightenment and the time travel chamber.

Sam still sported his walking cane, and while Ben looked a little rumpled, as if he'd slept in his baggy old clothes on the flight from New York, Claire looked as bright and cheerful as ever.

"I think the ring goes well with the smile," Dr. Weiss finished.

"Thank you," Claire replied as she dropped the hand she had been displaying. "And Ben helped me update my wardrobe while we were in New York. Though I must say, I don't know what people see in those pantsuit things. A lady can look nice and be a professional at the same time, don't you think?"

Ben grinned. "You won't hear any argument from me."

Their steps brought them to another hall perpendicular to their own. A digital clock on the wall displayed the time —7:00 p.m. on Friday— and to the right of it a sign pointed in the direction of security, while another, pointing left, was labeled section 2b. They were just coming up to the intersection when two people walked out from the right, one of whom all of them knew quite well. It was Special Agent Hessman, and by his side, Samantha, rubbing her shoulder.

"Lou!" Claire brightly exclaimed. "It's been too long."

She immediately skipped over and wrapped her arms around him for a quick hug before breaking off with a smile, her ring finger once again brought up for display.

"Look what Ben got me. Oh, I hope you'll be the best man when it's time."

Agent Hessman glanced down at the ring, then gave her an efficient smile as the others joined them.

"Congratulations, and I hope you have been acclimating well to our century, Miss Hill," he replied.

"I think that's about as close to an emotional reaction as you're going to get out of him," Ben said, grinning.

Nevertheless, Agent Hessman reached out to briefly shake Ben's hand, while Dr. Weiss stepped up to make the introductions.

"This is Samantha, my niece, a very bright girl that we're all quite proud of. Samantha, this is Professor Ben Stein and Claire Hill."

"The girl from the past," Samantha said as she reached out a hand to shake. "Lou here was getting me up-to-date with all the team members while my security chip was being implanted. My arm still stings."

Claire took the hand for a quick greeting as she replied, "They did that to me as well before we left. It faded away after about ten minutes, so don't worry."

"Lou has been showing me around the place, and I must say, I'm very impressed. I can only imagine how you're taking it."

Here Claire briefly giggled as Dr. Weiss led the way down the remaining hallway. "I'm impressed by things you consider outdated," she replied. "Like those things you record moving pictures on."

"CDs?"

"Actually, I was thinking of the tapes. And digital watches, and electric toothbrushes . . . Oh, I could go on all day."

"Our little vacation was a bit eye-opening for the both of us," Ben stated as he slid an arm around her waist. "There are some things I never really appreciated until seeing them through the eyes of someone a century out-of-date. But tell us a little about yourself, Samantha. You're joining the team?"

"I was on my way here when the attack came," Samantha replied.

To Ben's questioning look, Agent Hessman supplied a quick answer. "Group of Russians with some odd weapons. I'm still trying to track them down. That's why we had to end your trip a bit early."

"Oh my!" Claire exclaimed. "I hope it wasn't anything serious. Oh, of *course* it is, or we wouldn't be here right now."

"Sam was just giving us a little walking tour of the new upgrades," Ben put in.

"Sounds like something I need to listen in on," Samantha agreed. "Lead on, Uncle Sam."

The corridor Dr. Weiss was leading them down had grown increasingly busy with the coming and going of base personnel from one adjoining doorway or branching hall or another. They seemed to be walking down a main thoroughfare deeper into the heart of the facility.

"Since my niece hasn't bragged about herself yet, allow me to do it for her," Dr. Weiss began. "One of the youngest PhDs in physics that you'll ever meet, absolutely brilliant, and a budding expert on the theory of time travel and its consequences."

"Only because Uncle Sam encouraged me so much growing up. Now I'm a member of this project and soon to see an actual *working* time machine. Color me impressed."

"Don't let her fool you," Dr. Weiss continued. "She's brilliant. Even got on a think tank over at Caltech. What was that on, Sam?"

"Climate change," she replied. "But let's see more of this base."

"And what about that cane?" Ben asked. "How long until you'll be running around without it?"

"Actually, I'm thinking of keeping it. Makes for a rather stylish look, don't you think?"

"Back in my time all the gentlemen sported canes," Claire put in. "That and a top hat."

"I'm not too sure about the hat," Dr. Weiss replied. "Then I'd have to get a suit to go along with it. Anyway, in the months since you two went on your trip, there have been a few upgrades. First, we've enhanced the monitoring of TDWs to better pinpoint the time and location of the events, as well as to allow for quicker detection. All the better to prevent any changes to history."

They came to a four-way intersection. The middle hall was labeled time chambers, the right command, and the left medical. Ben noted the plural form of the first sign and eyed Dr. Weiss.

"Yes, we had a second chamber constructed," Sam replied. "That way we can respond to multiple temporal events. The general has also increased the reaction teams to three to respond on a moment's notice. One for each chamber and a backup."

"Sounds like a wise precaution," Samantha remarked, "but has anyone considered the ramifications of having two temporal chambers operating simultaneously? Two wormholes so close to one another might have some crossover effects."

"We've been running some simulations and tests, and so far all looks okay," Dr. Weiss replied. "We just have to keep their dimensional operating frequencies sufficiently separated."

He turned down the left hall toward Medical and continued his explanations.

"I have also been working on developing a temporal neutral field that will surround each chamber so that all within them will be immune to any changes to history that may be incurred during a trip—at least in theory. We haven't had a chance to test it out yet, and we hope we'll never really need it."

"That's Uncle's way of saying it may still have a few bugs in it," Samantha said. "But I have faith in him."

"It's one of the reasons why I recommended that my niece join the team. Her input will help me fine-tune a few things. We also vastly increased the data storage of the computers in these protected areas so as to hold as much data on world history as can possibly be found. After our first excursion it was decided that every detail, no matter how small, could turn out to be very important."

"I know one of those little details saved *my* life," Claire put in. "Though I wish I could have at least said goodbye to my parents."

Ben saw the brief look of regret on her face and hugged her closer as they walked.

"At any rate, the purpose of all these changes is to add a more proactive operation to ensure that others do not disrupt history, while also allowing the safe and supervised observation of historical events."

Both the tour and their steps came to a halt before the central nursing station of the circular hub that was the medical section. Ringed around it was a series of partitions leading into the adjoining patient rooms, with one at the opposite side labeled "OR." They paused here for a moment, with a couple of questioning looks directed at Dr. Weiss.

"Phelps didn't make it," Dr. Weiss said to the unvoiced question. "We lost him just the other day."

"And Sue?" Claire asked.

Sam said nothing, just led them around to the left, past two partitions. At the third he parted the curtain and let Claire and Ben proceed inside. Behind them Samantha was about to step forward, but a gentle hand from Agent Hessman stopped her. He simply gave her a look to which she replied with a nod.

Agent Sue Harris, a black lady with short-cropped hair, was wired up with tubes and sensors, surrounded by monitor devices to one side and a medical drip to the other. Her eyes were closed, and if the slow progression of her heart rate being displayed on one of the monitors was any indication, she would remain unconscious for some time to come. Seeing her like this, Claire found herself clutching Ben's hand tightly as the two approached the edge of the bed.

Ben and Claire

"Sue," Claire whispered. "Hey, sorry I haven't been in to see you in a while, but Ben's been showing me around. I wish you could have been up to come along with us. There was a pair of would-be muggers that I would have loved to see you take care of."

A tear drifted down Claire's cheek, accompanied by a forced smile, as she reached out to lightly caress the unconscious lady's hand. Then she remembered what was on her own hand and brought it up before Sue's face as if she might see it.

"Look what Ben got me. We're engaged now. Oh, he's made me just so happy. I always felt a little out of place back when I came from, but around Ben . . . I never thought my dreamboat would come from another time. At any rate, I want you to be my maid of honor, so we'll hold off the wedding however long it takes until you're awake and can attend."

She drew back her hand and leaned in close to whisper in Agent Harris's ear. "But you better wake up real soon because I really want to marry this guy."

It was a few moments longer before Ben and Claire came out of the room to rejoin Dr. Weiss. Claire sniffed sadly as she glanced up and happened to see Lou and Samantha across the room. They were idly conversing, Samantha with a pleasant smile, Agent Hessman with his usual noncommittal composure. In Claire's view, however, his emotional neutrality seemed just a little forced when around Samantha, and to this Claire flashed a grin as they followed Dr. Weiss out of the medical wing.

They found themselves soon enough back at the previous intersection, this time headed down the hall labeled command, with Dr. Weiss once again narrating.

"The command center has seen several upgrades, as you'll see, but the most important one is General Karlson himself."

"General Karlson?" Ben asked. "What happened to him?"

"Did he become a mechanical man or something?" Claire asked. "Because in this time I never know just what may be possible."

"Nothing as extreme as that, Miss Hill," Agent Hessman replied. "He has simply been promoted to four-star general."

General Karlson

As they approached a heavy security door, a pair of armed security men eyed them carefully. The walls to either side of the door had what looked like a glass surface, and as they each walked between them the glass flashed green. Only then did the guards relax as the security door began to slide open.

"Weight sensors in the floor to tell when there's anyone here," Agent Hessman explained, "coupled with the wall sensors scanning for those security chips everyone's been implanted with. If it senses a weight and no accompanying chip signal, then the panels flash red and things get a little messy."

"I'm just impressed by the fact that the gate is sliding aside all by itself," Claire remarked. "The rest is just gravy."

Once the thick metal door had slid fully aside, Dr. Weiss led the way through.

4

LITTLE MYSTERIES

The command room had been expanded: there was a sea of stations below the general's command platform, across from which the far wall now held a larger TDW Location Board, or simply "blip board" as many there would call it. General Karlson stood at his station with Captain Beck beside him, the former greeting them all with a nod, to which Samantha replied with a respectful enough word or two, though Claire wasn't letting him off that easy. But she flung her arms around Captain Beck, crying out, "Robert!" then switched to hugging the general before he could object. A moment later she eased back with a shy grin.

"Sorry, but it *was* your people that cured me and you that allowed me to stay in this time."

"Quite understandable, Miss Hill, just"—the general lowered his voice for her ears alone—"not in front of the men, if you please."

Claire backed off with a quick curtsey, then stepped back alongside Ben as the general shifted his attention.

"Dr. Samantha Weiss, I believe," he said, putting out a hand. "You come very highly recommended. Nice to meet you. I'm General Karlson and this is Captain Beck."

"Another member of the first team," she replied. "Yes, my uncle told me all about you."

"I'm the old man of the team," Captain Beck said with a brief flash of a grin. "I understand your trip was a bit less than uneventful."

"A brief ruckus, which Lou here handled quite admirably," Samantha stated. "I think I would feel perfectly safe anywhere he's around."

"Agent Hessman is one of our top men," the general replied, oblivious to the sly smile she was now giving Agent Hessman. "Agent Hessman, I believe you have a report to make about that incident."

During this, Claire had been slowly panning the room with wonder-filled eyes, taking in everything from simple flat-panel monitors and winking lights to the vast screen on the opposite wall. Occasionally she would smile in delight at one object or another, until her gaze happened to take in the look that Samantha was giving Agent Hessman and the way Hessman was maintaining his composure. Then she quietly giggled but said nothing.

"I am most eager to get to work," Samantha told them. "I suppose now is as good a time as any to announce this. Uncle Sam and I have been working on something together."

"A new theory," Dr. Weiss eagerly broke in. "You might even call it astounding."

"Oh really?" the general said with a curious look. "What sort of theory?"

Dr. Weiss looked like a kid busting out with a secret, but despite his own obvious eagerness, he gave the nod to his niece, who immediately jumped in.

"We believe that it should be possible to move *forward* in time as well."

"Technically," Claire put in, "I already did."

"Forward from the perspective of the time machine, of course," Dr. Weiss supplied. "Now, as you can well imagine, this raises several questions."

"Like, forward into *which* future?" Ben asked. "Is the future already written, or are we talking one of several possibilities? And would you be able to change the future if it really hasn't happened yet? And how would you do that?"

"Sam and I have been having this debate for weeks now," Dr. Weiss replied. "I think it's a matter of each possible future having a certain quantum probability of coming to pass depending on the unfolding of current events."

"Which means that technically you aren't changing the future," Samantha stated, "so much as aligning the current present with one of the probable futures. Now, as far as bringing something back with you from the future, there might be some danger involved. For instance, doing so could change the present and hence put you on a path to a different future in which that object you brought back with you might not even exist anymore, or at least not in that form."

"Philosophical quandaries are ever the prospect of time travel," Ben put in, "forward *or* back. We discovered for ourselves the problems with changing the past. Would there be something similar involving the future?"

"Possibly," Dr. Weiss thoughtfully replied. "We can't really change the past, at least not the big events. But if we're part of someone else's past, then they would have the same trouble trying to effect changes in *our* present to affect *their* present, which would be their future; but since we haven't picked our own future yet, then would we have more power to effect such a change if stimulated by visitors from a given future?"

"Again," Ben stated, "which future? You're making it sound like we could have visitors from any of several different futures. And if we go to visit one possible future, does that then lock us onto a path to that one alone?"

Claire's eyes were starting to glaze over, and Captain Beck was massaging his temples, though Agent Hessman remained expressionless and General Karlson looked annoyed.

"I think it boils down to this," Samantha stated. "We'll have many of the same problems going forward as going back. However, if someone can be convinced in their own native timeline to do something that may affect their future, then in that way a traveler from the future may be able to effect a change, though they would have to be very careful in how they proceeded."

"Agreed," Dr. Weiss replied.

"Though I wonder," Samantha continued, "if, as a result of traveling to the future, one might come back with no memory of the experience so as to protect the integrity of the future timeline."

"Something put down by the powers that be?" Ben asked. "That sounds a little theological to me."

"And a discussion for another time," Claire quickly broke in. "Speaking as the only one here who has been and continues to exist in my own future, I can tell you that my head hurts just thinking about it, and General Karlson looks like he's been trying to get your attention for the last five minutes now."

"What? Oh, sorry, General," Dr. Weiss said. "We can really get into it at times."

"So I noticed," the general replied. "Lou, you were about to make a report."

Attention now shifted to Agent Hessman, who went into his report with far less philosophical sidetracking than was in the previous discussion.

"Los Alamos caught our attention because this is the second time that a conference on time travel has been attacked, only this time the attackers vanished before our very eyes. I've scoured the site for clues and only found these."

He reached into a pocket and brought out some shell casings and presented them to the general.

"The lab boys tell me these are unlike anything currently manufactured and, in fact, are not regular bullets. From what they can tell, these things are guided and appear to be designed to explode in an electrical burst on impact. No real damage, but enough to heavily stun the target."

"Like a Taser but without wires," General Karlson said.

"Exactly so."

"But who could make such a thing?"

"We heard then speaking Russian," Dr. Weiss put in.

"Russians." General Karlson took the bullets, looking at them thoughtfully before replying. "Does this mean that the Russians are trying to kidnap a few scientists to construct their own chamber? The problem is, though, that I can confirm that bullets such as these are not even on the drawing board for either us *or* Russia . . . Lou, has everyone been chipped?"

"The last of base personnel should be going through it now," Agent Hessman replied. "Ben and Claire were chipped before I'd let them leave the base."

"I still remember the sting," Ben quipped. "These chips . . ."

"With them we can track base personnel anywhere on the planet with the help of our satellites," General Karlson explained. "After our new funding came through, I started it with certain key personnel, but after this latest incident I had Agent Hessman chip everyone down to the janitorial staff. Okay, Lou, I want you to keep any eye out for these Russians. Samantha Weiss, I believe you have a new lab to get to. And Miss Hill . . . I have a surprise for you."

He reached back to one of the computer stations ringed immediately around him to pick up a folder lying there and handed it to Claire.

"May I present you with your new identity, Miss Hill. Birth certificate, Social Security card, and other documentation as proclaims you a resident of *this* century. Welcome *officially* to the twenty-first century, Miss Hill."

Claire's face bloomed like a dawning sunrise as, with shaking hand, she timidly took the folder, the gratitude welling up in her eyes, to which the general immediately raised a hand before her.

"No hugs. I'll take that look as thanks enough."

"I don't know where to begin," Claire replied.

"Just memorize everything as soon as you can, Miss Hill."

"I will. Oh, I . . . But if I may ask . . . What's a Social Security card?"

The question took everyone off guard and had Samantha breaking out into a grin.

"I'll explain it to her," Ben offered.

"You do that," the general said a little gruffly. "Now, I believe every-one has some place to be."

"Miss Weiss . . . ," Agent Hessman began.

"Just call me Samantha."

"Samantha, if you will allow me to escort you to your lab, then."

"General, sir." It was a technician at one of the stations immediately behind the general; he was sporting an earpiece, and the monitor before him was displaying a fresh message. "We just got word from Medical. Agent Harris is awake."

"Sue!" Claire exclaimed.

She was the first to hurry out, with Ben fast on her heels along with Captain Beck, and Sam hobbling along behind them.

"Hey, wait up. I'm a cripple, remember."

Agent Hessman turned quickly to Samantha, but before he could say anything, she spoke first.

"I can find my way to my lab; you go see your friend."

A quick nod of gratitude and Agent Hessman was off to join the others. General Karlson would soon follow at a far more dignified pace.

5

HARRIS AWAKENS

The little room adjoining the nurses' station was soon packed with a small crowd of people rushing to get in. Claire and Ben arrived in the lead to see a nurse tending to a groggy Agent Harris, while behind them came Agent Hessman, Captain Beck, then Dr. Weiss using his cane to clear himself a way through. All of them wanted to crowd in around the bed, but the nursing staff had other ideas. Even when General Karlson himself finally came up, they would allow no more than Claire and Ben to enter; the rest would have to wait just outside, though with a clear view as the attending nurse worked the controls of the bed to move Agent Harris up into a close approximation of a sitting position.

"Sue, you're back with us!" Claire exclaimed.

Claire looked as if she were ready to crush Agent Harris beneath the weight of her eager welcome, but a look from the attending nurse and she relented with a light touch to her shoulders, to which Agent Harris replied with a very slow nod and weak smile.

"First question: What century is this?" Agent Harris asked slowly between breaths.

The others out in the hallway broke into relieved chuckles, though Agent Hessman kept a steady eye on every detail of Sue's appearance and apparent health.

"We're back in the present," Ben assured her. "The mission was a complete success, though we lost Phelps."

Sue bowed her head briefly at mention of Phelps, then looked back up to Claire. "I'm glad the mission worked out. But if I may ask, and don't take this the wrong way," she said slowly, "but what are you doing here?"

More smirks circulated the small crowd, not the least of which was from Claire as she answered the question.

"Ben brought me forward, then had the doctors fix me of my pneumonia. He saved my life."

Agent Harris noted how Claire looked up with such loving eyes to Ben by her side, and managed a weak chuckle.

"That's what I get for being unconscious for . . . How long have I been out, anyway?"

Before anyone could say anything, Claire simply brought up her hand with the ring and showed it to Sue with a wide grin on her face.

"*That* long," Sue replied. "Well, that's all *I* need to know for now. Congratulations."

"I want you to be my maid of honor," Claire announced. "Would you please?"

"I'd have drop-kicked anyone else that you would have asked." Sue weakly grinned. "Just as soon as I can hobble out of here."

"Hey," Dr. Weiss called in, "maybe we can have matching canes."

"Sam?" Sue said, looking up. "How'd you get up and around before me?"

"I didn't come riding in attached to a bomb." Dr. Weiss grinned.

"Oh yeah, I knew there was something unpleasant I'd been through. Looks like the rest of you made it. Sorry about Phelps, though."

"I'm glad you pulled through, Sue," Claire said. "I don't have too many friends in this century, after all."

To Ben's exaggerated throat-clearing, Claire glared in his direction. "You're my lover and betrothed, so that doesn't count," she said.

Sue chuckled at the remark, or rather tried to and ended up wincing briefly. That was when the attending nurse intervened.

"Okay, everybody out; generals too. Agent Harris needs to rest now."

"Some of us have some duties to get to anyway," Agent Hessman put in. "Welcome back, Agent Harris."

A chorus of well-wishes hit Agent Harris as the nurse shooed everyone away from the small room, then drew the partition across into place, cutting off view from the others.

Claire sighed. "Well, at least I can sleep better knowing she's going to be okay."

"I thought there was another reason why we weren't sleeping much," Ben quipped —a comment which earned him a light punch in the arm by Claire, while General Karlson called everyone back to order.

"Okay, everyone, back to your duty stations. Hessman, I want more on those Russians as soon as you can."

6

KIDNAPPING

While everyone else was visiting a recovering Agent Harris, Samantha was tracking down her new lab. She walked down the nearest corridor and found a terminal mounted on the wall. No keyboard, just a simple touchscreen displaying a map of the base.

"Hmm," she muttered to herself, "I wonder if this thing is voice activated. Uh, Dr. Samantha Weiss. I'm looking for my lab and how to get there."

Immediately the map changed, first indicating her current location with a large red dot, then expanding while a red line ran through the maze of displayed hallways until it reached a destination and another dot lit up. Everything else on the map then grayed out save the suggested route to her lab.

"Nice."

She studied the map for a few moments, then tapped the screen, with a quick "Thank you," whereupon the display returned to the general map display it had been before.

Samantha started walking again, this time making a right at the first intersection of corridors she came to, per the instructions from the display. Along the way she passed two lab-coated scientists engaged in their own discussion, one soldier who gave her a polite nod in passing, and a confused-looking technician reading the labels of the doors he passed, hoping to find the right one.

When the hallway ended at another hall perpendicular to hers, one wall of which sported an elevator, she went straight to the elevator, took out her ID card, and flashed it before the sensor. A moment later the doors opened and she was inside looking at a short panel of buttons. She pressed one of them, the doors closed, and she began to descend.

"I'll admit, Lou's kinda cute," she said to herself. "And smart. I like a man with a brain. I wonder if he likes women with IQs of one hundred fifty."

One level down the elevator came to a stop, the doors opened, and she was once again out in a fresh intersection. A glance up at the hallway labels to be certain and she took the direction ahead of her. The sign read, "L4." A short walk later she was standing before a sliding security door with a sensor next to it. A sign above the door simply read, "Temporal Physics—4."

"This must be the place."

A flash of her badge across the sensor opened the door. She then stepped inside for a look at the new lab, the door easing shut behind her.

The room was festooned with lab benches and computer stations. The far right wall supported a couple of man-sized pieces of experimental equipment whose function might be known solely to herself and the other lab techs, while the left wall was adorned with a thick glass window that looked out over a large testing chamber. Fifty feet across to the other side of the room was an open passage into what she assumed to be the break room. The room was silent, the only sound being the occasional beep from one of the terminals.

She walked in, looking around for any sign of life, and called out, "Hello? I'm doctor Samantha Weiss, but you can call me Sam." *They must be in the break room.*

She crossed the room, passing by one of the benches along the way, on which one of the terminals was blinking "Password Correct, Press to Continue."

"That's odd," she muttered. "That could be a security breach, just walking away from an open terminal like that."

For the moment she shrugged it off and kept walking, but once past the bench she saw something on the floor that caught her more suspicious glare: a spilled mug of juice, its contents pooling on the floor.

She immediately cast her gaze about, knees bending in a slight crouch. Carefully bending down, she picked up the mug. Then, holding it like a weapon, she rose back up and more carefully approached the break room, this time not saying a word, her steps silent.

The break room had no door, just an open partition in which she paused. She didn't go in, but rather stepped first to the left side for a better angle, then the right. From the right she could see a couple of chairs, part of a table with a microwave and coffeemaker, and two sets of legs lying on the floor.

She backed one slow step away, turned very deliberately, then, eyeing her course, bolted into a run. She was halfway across the lab when she saw what looked like a roughly man-sized shimmering appear before the door. She immediately stopped.

"I think I've seen this movie."

Taking the mug, she hurled it as hard as she could at the shimmering outline as she broke again into a run. The mug bounced off the air a couple of feet from the door, accompanied by a curse in a deep male voice, but the shimmering outline remained in place.

A few yards away from the door and the suspicious glimmering, and without warning, Samantha suddenly dropped to the floor on all fours, her back arched. Just as expected, she felt a moving weight slam into her side, letting out another male cry, as the invisible figure launched over her and into the one by the door, where it, too, briefly glimmered as the pair made contact.

"That's what I thought," she muttered as she leaped back up to her feet.

Wasting not a second, she swung around, grabbed the keyboard before the screen with the blinking cursor, then nearly pole-vaulted over to the other side, spilling papers and equipment along the way. Landing on her feet, she immediately began swinging the keyboard around like a weapon.

"I can't see you, but I'm guessing you're the same bunch that attacked us at Los Alamos. They had a way of vanishing before our eyes too."

A slight noise directed her attention, and spinning around, she swung the keyboard hard just in time to intercept something whizzing through the air. Something like a bullet hit the keyboard, projecting an electric charge into it that earned a burnt electric odor from within it.

She couldn't see where it had come from, but she could judge trajectories pretty well and immediately hurled the keyboard straight ahead of her. A few feet away it bounced off the air, earning a glittering display of light around a man-shaped figure. Samantha immediately charged forward, one fist flying, her other hand clawing across what she judged to be about head level. Her fist met hard flesh, while her open hand caught on to cloth, then yanked.

A hood tore loose, revealing the head of a man now seemingly afloat in the air. Samantha emitted a reflexive gasp and leaped back, her eyes darting from him to where the shimmering outlines by the door might now be.

"I guess that explains how you got in here in the first place, but what are you after? And why did you kill those two techs?"

She backed up against a table, one hand reaching back to brace herself and landing discreetly on a terminal keyboard.

"No one dead," the one before her said in a thick Russian accent. "We don't want to harm you."

Behind her back her fingers started working the keys, but before she could even begin stalling for time, another electrified bullet hit the keyboard, sending sparks flying and a startled Samantha leaping quickly away. This was followed by a third round hitting her in the neck from behind, the bullet, which now looked like a dart, sending her body into brief convulsions before she dropped limply to the floor, the man's hood dropping from her grip.

One of the shimmering figures that had been behind her now reached out a hand past the cloaking of invisibility and into full view. A hand holding a small round object that the figure reached down to place on the unconscious woman's chest. It looked like little more than a disk with a single large red button in its center, which the hand now pressed before quickly drawing back.

A shimmering of a different sort now enveloped Samantha's limp form. Rainbow lights outlined her more brightly by the instant, then were gone in an abrupt flash□ —along with Samantha herself.

The floating head muttered something in Russian, one of the other unseen figures responding with a chuckle; then he retrieved his hood from where Samantha had dropped it and put it back on, once again becoming for the most part unseen. A moment later the three shimmering figures were surrounded in their own auras of rainbow lights. A flash, then nothing remained behind.

Nothing save a pair of unconscious techs and signs of a struggle, including one fried keyboard with a strange bullet embedded in it.

7

VANISHED

The clocks read 8:30 p.m. when the alarm went off across the base. Soldiers hurried to their duty stations. Ben and Claire looked briefly confused before Ben decided to lead the way quickly back to the command center, passing up a hobbling Dr. Weiss along the way, while Agent Hessman was already running down the final stretch into the command center, an earpiece in his ear via which he was calling out orders to other personnel.

"Sam," Ben asked as they approached, "what's going on?"

"I have no idea," the man replied. "Go on ahead, I'll catch up."

"Here, allow me."

Hurrying up behind them came Captain Beck. He took Dr. Weiss by one arm and nodded to the other pair. "I'm old and slow anyway," he remarked. "You two see what's going on."

So, while Ben and Claire hurried on, Captain Beck did his best to bring up Dr. Weiss's pace.

When the first pair burst into the command center, they saw Agent Hessman directing something from one of the terminals on the central command platform, while General Karlson was issuing his own orders.

"Lock down the entire base," the general was saying as they came in. "Not so much as a mouse gets in or out."

As Ben and Claire approached, still confused, they could hear Agent Hessman's commands to his security teams via his terminal and earpiece.

"Last known location was her lab. I want it searched, as well as all adjoining corridors. Call up security footage from both the lab and attached halls. Heck, call it up for any adjacent areas whether they have access into that lab or not. I'm not discounting the possibility that these people can burrow through walls at this point."

Claire was first to voice the question as their steps brought her and Ben to a stop at the edge of the platform: "What's going on?"

Agent Hessman spun up to his feet; then seeing Captain Beck and Dr. Weiss just entering at the back, he gave a look to the general. General Karlson replied with a nod, to which Agent Hessman began his brief report.

"Samantha's location chip just went off-line. No sign of it anywhere."

"My niece," Dr. Weiss gasped, his hobble increasing in pace, "what's happened to her? Has she been hurt? Oh my God."

"Samantha," Claire gasped.

"As close as I can figure, she hasn't died," Agent Hessman reported. "The chips are designed to give off a different signal if the person has died. And if the chip itself were somehow damaged, there would have been a sign of impending failure in the signal, however brief that might've been. For both cases we have nothing."

"Nothing?" Dr. Weiss said as he stumbled onto the command platform with Captain Beck's help. "But how can you have nothing?"

"I'm saying that there is no trace of it anywhere. The signal simply stopped. Her lab and room are being searched, but so far we have— Hold on."

He tapped a finger to his earpiece to listen, while even the general waited to hear the result.

"Okay," Agent Hessman said into the air, "keep up the search and lock everything down. Guards at every intersection."

Removing his finger from his earpiece, he turned to face the general. Dr. Weiss of course displayed the worried concern of a doting uncle, but behind Agent Hessman's professional exterior Claire could see another concerned look, though not because of any familial relationship.

"Well?" the general snapped. "Who was it, and how'd they get into my base?"

"Samantha's two techs were found unconscious in their lab break-room," Agent Hessman reported. "There are signs of a struggle, in which my team also found two bullets."

"Sam!" Dr. Weiss gasped.

"The same odd electrified bullets we found at the Los Alamos conference incident."

General Karlson nodded. "Those Russians again. But how did they get in here?"

"The lab security footage may give us a clue. I have it ready to play."

"I thought the security cams were only in the corridors," Ben said.

"The ones you'll find on record," Agent Hessman admitted. "Because of what we do here, every bit of lab space is monitored by one or more security cameras about the size of your fingertip. Even the placement of the cameras is encrypted."

"Sounds a bit paranoid," Claire remarked.

"Just be glad that I am."

"Play the footage up on the big screen, Hessman," the general ordered.

To the general's command, Agent Hessman reached to his terminal, hit a few keys, and then faced the large screen on the front wall along with everyone else.

The footage first showed the two techs suddenly dropping to the ground, their bodies then being dragged into the break room by unseen means. After a pause it showed Samantha walking in. They watched as she walked across the room, bent down to pick up the mug, and then started running after eyeing the break room. They watched as the mug bounced off the air, and saw Samantha leap over one of the workbenches, use her keyboard to deflect one of the strange electrified bullets, and finally rip something off to reveal the head of a man afloat in the air.

"He's a ghost," Claire gasped.

"More likely some manner of adaptive camouflage cloth," Dr. Weiss remarked. "I've read of some experiments to develop this sort of technology, but nothing even close to this sort of sophistication."

The scene then came to when Samantha collapsed, then the disembodied hand reaching out to place the disk on her unconscious form. That's when Agent Hessman's eyes narrowed suspiciously and when Dr. Weiss went from concerned uncle to investigative research scientist. A moment later Samantha's body vanished in a prismatic twinkle, soon followed by three more such flashes.

"Stop the tape right there," Dr. Weiss called out. "I need a terminal and a copy of the last few seconds of Samantha's location signal to analyze."

"A suspicion, Doctor?" the general asked.

"More than mere suspicion," he replied. "I think everyone on the team knows what that disk and flash of lights are reminiscent of."

Agent Hessman nodded, and said, "Agreed. General, I'd like to scan for any TDWs in the last twenty-four hours."

"Do it," the general ordered the nearest tech.

While Dr. Weiss sat down to work at one of the terminals, and Agent Hessman watched as the security footage was replaced by the readout from the TDW scanners, Captain Beck gently pulled Ben and Claire back a little from the center of activity.

"Let them do their work," he quietly told them. "Sam is more worried than you are about his niece, but he's focused now on locating her."

"I know," Ben replied, "but I feel so frustrated."

"And unexpectedly vulnerable," Claire added. "I thought this base was impregnable."

Captain Beck left the question unanswered as they turned their attention to the results now displayed across the main screen.

"Nothing on the blip board," a tech finally called out. "No TDWs going to or from the past."

"I didn't expect there would be," Agent Hessman said thoughtfully. "Sam?"

"In just a second . . ."

Dr. Weiss's fingers raced across his keyboard as he worked. On the screen before him was a waveform pattern displayed as a function of time codes, but under his swift work it zoomed into the last fractions of a second and expanded. Now the steady waveform was disrupted by a completely different pattern.

"We got a time traveler, all right," he announced. "See that disruptive pattern in the last instant of the signal? That's the locator signal being distorted by a time travel event. Look for a blip again, but this time from the *future*."

"Uh, Doctor?" the same tech who had reported the lack of TDWs asked. "But . . . how?"

Dr. Weiss started typing again as he spoke. "A little something that Sam and I have been working on. I'm feeding you the new parameters now. You just have to make a few adjustments."

While Dr. Weiss was sending the new information and the tech was making his adjustments, General Karlson stepped in next to Agent Hessman for a few quiet words.

"Russians from the future? Any idea why?"

"That attack at the Los Alamos conference must have been aimed for Samantha Weiss. She has something they need, though what I can't yet imagine. We won't know more until we're able to tell just how *far* into the future they come from."

"It would explain the odd tech they've displayed —electrified bullets, something that makes them invisible."

"Explains a lot," Agent Hessman agreed, "though not their motive."

Their short conference was interrupted by the tech calling out, "General, activity on the blip board. We have a TDW, and it's from the future, all right."

"Display it," the general snapped. "I want location and time."

"Yes, sir."

The large screen before them displayed first a black background, then a single large dot at one end accompanied by a time stamp. From there a line began drawing itself toward the other side of the screen, passing up briefly displayed date codes along the way. A short distance from the first dot, a second one appeared; from there the line started stretching all the way across the screen.

"From the looks of it," Dr. Weiss announced as he struggled to get up from his seat, "their first portal opened up this morning, in the vicinity of Los Alamos."

"Makes sense," the general remarked. "And do we have to guess the time of the second?"

"Right when my niece's locator chip went off-line. Right when that flash in the security footage showed her disappearing."

"Then, if I may," Ben said, stepping forward, "how far into the future are they from?"

"We'll know in a few moments," Dr. Weiss replied, "but judging on the tech they've displayed so far and the apparent ease with which they snuck in, I'd say nothing less than about fifty years, maybe more. It wouldn't have been from too far into the future, though, or they probably would have just teleported her out or something."

A glance up showed the line was already passing up the fifty-year mark.

"Well," Dr. Weiss said, a little nervously, "any bets as to exactly how far?"

"Lou," General Karlson said, "the second we have a date and location, I want you to assemble a team. No one kidnaps one of our people no matter *how* far in the future they come from."

"Yes, General."

"Sir," Dr. Weiss broke in, "I'd like to—"

"Sam, until you no longer need that cane, you're grounded," the general told him. "You'll be a liability in the field. I know she's your niece and you love her, but that's the way it has to be."

"I understand, sir. But can I at least run tech support from this end? I've got to do *something*."

"As long as it doesn't involve much more than you sitting in place and some light walking," the general agreed.

Dr. Weiss replied with a sigh of some little relief before the discussion was cut off by an announcement from the same tech as before.

"Sir, we have a date and location."

All eyes looked up at the blip board to see that a third dot had resolved at the far end of the screen, one displaying some text, which the tech now read off from his terminal.

"We pin it at one hundred years in the future. Location: London, England."

"England?" the general puzzled. "I would have expected Russians to be from Russia. And what's England doing with a time machine?"

"It could be like the nuclear bomb, sir," Ben put in. "It started out with just us and the Russians; then all the major powers started getting it."

"Quick aside," Claire said, "but what's a 'nuclear bomb'?"

"Oh yeah," Ben replied in a subdued tone, "I've been avoiding telling you about those. The first one erased an entire city."

"An entire *city*?" Claire gasped. "One bomb? What sort of warmongering madness are you people into, anyway?"

"Long story for another time, Miss Hill," Agent Hessman interjected. "Right now, we have Samantha to rescue."

"Right," she agreed. "Priorities."

"Now, we'll need someone to replace Agent Harris and Lieutenant Phelps," Agent Hessman began as he turned away, thinking. "There's a couple of people that I think might do the job . . ."

While Agent Hessman thought over the composition of the team, Claire pulled Ben away for a quiet word between them alone.

"He really likes her a lot."

"What, Sam's niece? She seems very personable, but—"

"No, I mean he *likes* her." She grinned.

"What? Oh. But what makes you think that?"

"Simple," she said with a shrug. "He keeps referring to her as 'Samantha' instead of 'Miss Weiss.' He's known me longer and I'm still 'Miss Hill' most of the time. Yep, he's got it bad."

Ben puzzled over this for a few moments, and as he watched Agent Hessman work quickly at getting his team together, he could not help but wonder if that was from his usual efficiency or some new urgency that arose from a completely different reason.

Temporal Chamber Control Room

Temporal Chamber

8

MISSION TO THE FUTURE

By nine o'clock Agent Hessman had his team assembled in the temporal projection chamber, unofficially known as "The Bubble." The pods were still ringed around the center beneath the two large curved propeller arms attached to the polished metal ball. The wires overhead had been cleaned up for a more professional look, and the control booth looking down upon it all had been greatly expanded, including the moving of the bulk of the computers from the Bubble's floor into the control booth. The general was already up in the booth, along with Dr. Weiss, while Agent Hessman was on the floor with the rest of the team.

He started his briefing while the techs went about a last check of the pods and the other equipment in the chamber.

"The team will be comprised of myself, Captain Beck, and Professor Stein," he began, "along with two new faces. First we have Master Chief Petty Officer Marvin Duke."

The man indicated was a well-built, clean-cut twenty-eight-year-old, around six feet two, who looked as if he could bench-press a small jeep. He replied with a quick nod and stated, "Just call me Chief Duke."

The next one that Agent Hessman indicated looked more like a picture of a man than the real thing: dark hair trimmed short, nondescript business suit, and dark glasses, with a face that displayed about as much emotional inflection as the suit he wore.

"And this is Agent Stevens. He's filling in for Agent Harris while she recovers."

"Nice to meet you," Ben stated, putting out a hand. "And what should we call you?"

The man's reply was as terse as his appearance: "Agent Stevens." He made no move to return Ben's offered hand or even acknowledge that it existed.

"I see," Ben said hesitantly.

"Agent Stevens is more of your classic spook," Captain Beck told him. "Won't give his first name unless ordered by the president himself, and I have my doubts that's even his real last name."

"I am here to do a job," Agent Stevens stated. "I will do my best to perform as efficiently as Agent Harris would have."

"Nothing personal," Claire spoke up, "but you'll never be as good as Sue."

"Nevertheless," Agent Hessman remarked, "he is the best available replacement that I could get on such short notice. Which brings up a pertinent question: Miss Hill, what are you doing here?"

"I'm going on the mission with the rest of you," she announced.

Agent Stevens was dressed in his suit, Chief Duke in army fatigues, Captain Beck in a gray business suit, Ben in the relaxed trousers and long-sleeved corduroy shirt that a university professor might wear, which is to say his own clothes, and Agent Hessman in a generic collared shirt and jacket and jeans. Claire, however, was attired far sprightlier, in an ankle-length pink-and-white dress, with a ribbon-scarf around her neck and a wide-brimmed, floppy white sunhat.

"Dressed like that?" Captain Beck remarked. "That doesn't exactly blend in, you know."

"Oh? And how would you know?" Claire countered. "How many people in this room have been to the future?" She immediately raised her own hand, then glanced around at everyone else keeping theirs down.

"Miss Hill, you are still in the present," Agent Hessman reminded her.

"Your present, but *my* future. None of us have any idea what the dress and customs might be a hundred years from now. For all we know, what I'm wearing right now could be the in style, while that business suit of Agent Stevens's is considered gauche. We're all in the same bucket on this one, only I have an advantage. *I've* actually had experience in adapting to new futuristic circumstances, new ways and customs. Anybody here also have that same experience?"

"She does have a point, Agent Hessman," Agent Stevens emotionlessly replied.

"Thank you, Fred," Claire said.

"The name's Agent Stevens, ma'am."

"Well, I'd like to call you by your first name, but since you won't give it, I've decided on Fred. Unless you *would* like to give us your first name to use?"

Agent Stevens said nothing.

"Fred it is." Claire triumphantly grinned.

Ben found himself suppressing a snicker, while Claire continued arguing her case.

"Besides, as a reporter, how can I pass up this opportunity? I'm also better trained at observing things and recording them for you."

"Another point in her favor, Lou," Captain Beck stated.

"Very well, Miss Hill," Agent Hessman said after a moment, "you can be a part of the team. Now, you've each been armed with a stun gun, some chloroform, and some English and American money in the off chance that they might still be using cash in the future. Also, your recall beacons, of course. Miss Hill, I shall have to requisition some equipment for you."

"Already done," she said with a bright grin. "I spoke with General Karlson earlier and got his approval using the same argument."

"Then why didn't you simply—"

"The general said I had to get your approval also, but since I knew that I probably would, I got equipped at the same time as Ben. Not too sure about those stun-gun things, though, but I'm ready to go."

"Well, then," Captain Beck remarked, "may I say that you do a good job of hiding everything? Because I can't see any sign of a single pistol bulge on you."

She shrugged. "A lady knows how to keep things under her hat. Now, are we ready?"

Agent Hessman let out a sigh, then looked toward Ben and said, "I do not envy you your coming married life with this woman, Professor."

"Yeah," Ben agreed, "let's hope I can keep up."

Captain Beck gave a light chuckle; Chief Duke, a level look; and from Agent Stevens, no sign that he felt anything.

"To continue," Agent Hessman said, picking up where they had left off, "the mission parameters are as follows: First and top priority is to bring back Samantha Weiss, alive and intact. Second is to find out why anyone from the future would want to kidnap her in the first place. Was it really the Russians? And if so, why are they apparently using a time machine in England? Then lastly, we are to observe and record this future, and if opportunity presents itself, bring back some samples."

"I'm not sure if that will be either possible or wise," Ben cautioned. "We may be disrupting our own timeline and what is to happen, or we may change our world, by just bringing something back with us."

"These people already violated that rule by kidnapping Samantha," Agent Hessman replied. "If they're trying to affect something in their past, then we can take advantage of a visit to our future. And if it turns out that, by some cosmic law, it's *not* possible to bring any technology back, then we'll find that out along the way. Until then, we have a duty before us. Now, are there any other questions?"

There were none save one from Agent Stevens.

"Just one: What are the orders regarding killing? They may be restricted from killing anyone from their own past, but we have no such limitation."

"That's a horrible question!" Claire exclaimed. "Why would we ever need to kill anyone?"

"It's a very apt question, Miss Hill, and I'm glad that Agent Stevens brought it up. We are here on a rescue mission, to find and retrieve one of our own through any means available. Our mission is not to kill. *But* if the need is absolutely necessary and there is no other way . . . then consider it a last resort."

"Understood," Agent Stevens stated.

"Now, one more thing."

From a pocket Agent Hessman drew out what looked like some sort of palm-sized computer with a small screen built in, and held it so they could all see it.

"This has been programmed to respond to Samantha's locator chip. However, it may not have the same range as it does here in our time."

"I thought those things could be detected anyplace on the planet," Ben said.

"With the help of some satellites," Agent Hessman responded. "Satellites which may or may not still exist or be in fully working order a century from now. Worst case, expect a range of between a quarter and a half mile."

He put the device back into his pocket, then turned away toward the raised circle of ready pods.

"Time to get into our pods, people. Just remember to be adaptable. There's no telling what sort of situation we'll find ourselves landing into."

"Probably in the middle of some highway," Ben remarked.

"Nah, the cars'll be flying," Captain Beck told him.

"According to what I remember hearing as a boy, they were sup-posed to be flying *now*," Ben countered. "I'm still betting on highways."

As each member of the team was led to a pod and strapped in by one of the technicians, a voice came over the room's speakers. Not General Karlson as one might expect, but Dr. Weiss.

"Please," he began, "bring back my niece. Whatever it takes."

"We will do our best, Dr. Weiss," Agent Hessman called out from within his pod.

Once everyone was strapped in and their pods sealed, the technicians cleared the pod platform, and everyone waited on the one person with the authority to make it all go. General Karlson took a last look at the chamber below, then at the men in their stations within his command booth, and seeing nothing in the way of red flags, he gave the word.

"Send them forward!"

Once again power surged through the mass of wiring down through the thick cabling to each of the pods to surround them with a brightening glow. High overhead the large twin propellers started to revolve, slowly at first, then picking up speed. As they did so a growing number of electrical sparks leapt between the blades and the mass of coiled wires above them. Faster and faster the blades spun, until they were a blur and the sparks filled the entire domed ceiling with a bright electrical haze. Soon nothing of the blades and wires could be seen, the domed ceiling now resembling a small star as the entire chamber resonated with power.

Then at the center of that star a dark eye opened, and from that black pupil the energy of Creation shot down the thick cables to the pods beneath, filling them each with a white glow.

"Just bring her back," Professor Weiss prayed from his spot in the control booth. "Please, bring her back."

9

LONDON, ENGLAND, 2120

They appeared in a flash inside a small room. Around them round boxes were stacked high and a variety of hats were scattered about, some in mid-completion on a workbench. To one end was a rear door, and at the other a cloth partition.

"We appear to be in a back room of some sort," Captain Beck remarked. "One with a lot of hats . . . A hatter?"

"London would be about the right type of place for it in any century," Ben agreed.

Agent Hessman crept over to the curtain for a quick peek. In the room beyond he saw a man measuring another man's head with a measuring tape. After creeping back to the others he said nothing, just pointed at the back door. Chief Duke led the way, opening the door a crack before walking out and holding it open for the rest. Only once outside would Agent Hessman allow anyone to talk.

"Okay, first thing, we get the lay of the land. The chamber would have deposited us as closely as it could to the TDW signal."

They found themselves standing in an alley, one as old and dirty as any alley of their own century.

Claire looked at some of the brown sludge along the edges and made a face. "Nothing new so far," she stated.

"Just don't touch anything until you're sure of what it is," Agent Hessman warned them all.

He led the way down the alley, pausing about halfway to what looked like a street. Before them, to one side of the alley, was a large metal box, nearly as tall as himself and twice that long and about three feet wide. He looked it over curiously, as did the others as they joined him. It looked like it had a lid across the whole top, which was currently closed and sealed shut.

"It looks like a garbage bin," Ben decided, "but I see what appears to be some sort of generator attached to one side. You don't find those on a garbage bin."

"Sir," Chief Duke said, bending forward to look at something on the front, "I found some writing. What looks like a model number and the words . . . 'flash can'?"

As they were puzzling over this, one of the other doors along the alley opened and a man hefting a large waste can in both hands came out. He came over to the large object, excused his way through the team, then kicked a spot at the base of the object. The object responded, the lid pivoting up, then from underneath it a mechanical arm reaching out with a pair of large metal pincers. The man placed his can on the ground before the object and stepped back a couple of feet while the pincers came down, clamped around the can, lifted it up overhead, tilted the can inward, dumped its contents, and then lowered the waste can back down before releasing it. As the arm and pincers withdrew, the man picked up his now-empty can and started walking back to his door. Meanwhile, the arms fully withdrew and the lid closed shut. A moment later a sudden flash of light was seen from the seam beneath the lid, accompanied by what sounded like a very large bug zapper.

"Flash can," Agent Hessman said with a knowing nod. "Futuristic trash can. It must disintegrate the trash on the spot."

"Sounds like an awful waste of energy just for getting rid of trash," Claire remarked.

"Depends how desperate you are to dispose of your trash," Ben told her.

"Enough of the back alley," Agent Hessman said. "Let's see what's out front."

Walking the rest of the way down the alley, they came at last onto an open street. It was a relatively small street a block down from what looked like a main artery of the city. As they stepped more fully out into the open, the true meaning of the word *futuristic* assaulted them all at once.

The city still had the classic mid-London architecture, the bulk of its buildings the combined product of the last few centuries, but there were clear signs scattered about them of a hundred years of upgrades. For one thing, while there were billboards atop some of the shorter buildings, in place of static flat pictures, these projected fully three-dimensional animated advertisements for one product or another, various businesses, and even the best candidate for prime minister. Flying through the air was something shaped roughly like a three-foot jet with a box attached to its underside. They watched as it flew right up to a fifth-story window, then hovered there. A moment later someone inside opened the window and reached out. The box then slid sideways on a small track from the little jet until the man had it firmly in hand. The jet then released the package and zoomed off into the sky.

The traffic filling the streets looked like sleek cars; they made no sound as they traveled save what the wheels made across the ground, and emitted no exhaust□ —they didn't even have tailpipes, for that matter□ —but they were unmistakably cars nonetheless. Along with them were what appeared to be taxis, one of which came to a stop in front of a man who had flagged it down. The odd thing was, though, the taxi had no driver that they could see. There were even the multilevel buses typical of London, each painted red, but once again lacking the roar of an engine and the usual exhaust pipe.

The traffic continued in the air above them as well. Not as many as were on the ground, but about a hundred feet above them lines of cars, with their wheels tucked in, were flying by way of miniature jets at their undersides and all around. They watched as one hopped up into the air from its parking space on the road below and joined the moving traffic, while a block down another one suddenly came to a halt and dropped quickly out of the traffic level onto the ground below, its wheels folding out as it came to a landing.

London 2120

London 2120

They walked slowly and cautiously along the sidewalk onto the main street, then stopped at a motion from Agent Hessman to observe more of what they could. A few doors down they saw a small storefront that was little more than an open service window topped by a menu featuring "Bangers and Mash." No one was operating it, however; rather, a set of robotic arms reached out and delivered the piping-hot cartons to the customers waiting just outside the window. Another shop featured gentlemen's clothing, but no mannequins were used to model its wares. Instead, they could see a holographic image in the window, turning this way and that just like a live person.

Finally, Agent Hessman spoke up: "A lot to take in, so stay together."

"What are we looking for?" Chief Duke asked.

"Something large and round," Agent Hessman answered. "I doubt that even a hundred years in the future a temporal chamber will have gotten reduced to palm sized, so it's going to stand out. We just need to get out from under these buildings for a better look at what's beyond."

"A newspaper," Claire suggested. "Even if time travel has become more publicly known, it'd still be the stuff of headlines."

"She's right," Ben agreed, "though I doubt the media of the day will involve actual printed paper."

"Oh posh," she replied. "I'll recognize a good newspaper no matter what form it's in."

"Is that a bet?" he asked.

Claire just smiled and then set a brisk pace down the street, the others forced to follow quickly along in her wake.

"Uh, sir," Chief Duke said in an aside to Captain Beck, "should Miss Hill be leading the way?"

"Well," the man said, shrugging, "one direction pretty much being as good as another under the circumstances, Claire has a proven talent for tracking down information, not to mention a remarkable amount of adaptability. Me, I'm still taking in everything we're seeing around here. So . . . go with it."

"Yes, sir. Had to check, sir."

That said, Chief Duke made sure to keep a pace behind Claire and Ben, his eyes on anyone coming within a couple of yards of them. Behind him walked Captain Beck and Agent Hessman, and behind them a wary-looking Agent Stevens.

It looked to be about midday, the streets crowded with vehicles, the walkways with a regular flow of pedestrians. It was hard to tell the exact time of day, though, the sky being overcast and threatening rain, with errant patches of fog littered about. From time to time an unexpected gust of wind came charging down the road, blowing away the lingering fog only to drop to a dead calm moments later. The people they passed sported a range of appearances as well, from a variation on the classic pants and dresses to something more extreme.

One young woman wore clear plastic pants, the only coloring they had being around her crotch, while her blouse looked like a curtain of shredded strips of blue cloth that somehow managed to stay bunched together enough to hid her nipples. Alongside her walked a young man with heavy boots, brown shorts, and a top hat and tie, the only other thing protecting him from the cold being not a shirt but a red cape that fell loosely back from his shoulders. Another lady was wearing what might best be described as an outline of a pair of blue jeans, topped by a T-shirt that emitted a hologram from a pair of bare breasts flashing on and off as she walked. Another man, though, seemed to take the opposite extreme of these others, wearing a colorful orange bodysuit that reached from his feet up to his neck, topped by a heavy white overcoat on the back of which was printed a large red rose with a small white star in the middle.

"I dare say that fashion sense has sunk even lower than in the twenty-first century," Claire remarked.

"Easily explained, Miss Hill," Agent Hessman said from behind them. "Notice that all the more radical fashions are worn by the young, people not past their twenties. The rebellious. Every generation has them."

As much as they could not help but stare oddly at the dress of the local youth, Agent Hessman noticed a few of them staring right back.

Captain Beck saw the reason for his concern and slipped in an observation to his companion.

"They may find our apparel just as odd as we find theirs."

"Perhaps," Agent Hessman hesitantly agreed, "but I see enough clothing styles at the other end of the spectrum to know that we should be fitting in pretty well. Even Miss Hill's hat should remain unnoticed."

"Then why the glances? Not many, but still."

"I . . . I don't know."

The street came up to another intersection, this one very large with a circle of cars going in and out of it instead of straight across. From there they could see two things of significance. To their left the road slanted down to a large river, but from what they could see of it, a long ten-foot-high wall ran the length of its coast, any access to the docks beyond being by way of an elevated bridge over it. The wall looked wide and was made not of bricks but of heavy stones and compressed earth.

"That looks like a dike," Ben remarked as they came to a stop. "But what's a dike doing along the river Thames?"

To their right the road reached out toward the unmistakable skyline of buildings that one would associate with a university. Classic ancient buildings, in their midst a brilliant star to crown it all that looked like a far more modern domed structure.

"That's London University," Ben announced. "I've been there once or twice. But that domed structure in the middle is new."

"How new?" Agent Hessman asked. "When was the last time you were in London?"

"About a hundred and two years ago."

Beside him Claire could not help but giggle.

"Sorry, couldn't resist. Two years ago, our time," Ben stated. "There was no sign of anything like that going up."

"Then we have one possible suspect target," Agent Hessman decided. "It's certainly about the right size and shape for a temporal chamber, but let's not presume anything just yet."

"Ah, there we are."

Claire was indicating a public kiosk of some sort a few yards away. One man was just leaving it, the screen he'd been looking at blanking out.

"And if I may ask, what makes you think this qualifies as a newspaper?" Ben asked.

"Public access, street corner, and that man was just looking at some moving pictures the way you guys do on those terminals of yours," she replied. "What else *could* it be? Though I didn't see him putting any money in. Maybe it's free."

With that, she walked over to the kiosk, though leaping up from behind her came Chief Duke.

"Excuse me, ma'am," he said, putting an arm out before her, "but there could be a danger. That's a computer terminal."

"Is that what newspapers look like in the future?" she asked. "Well, let's see what's been going on."

Before he could say otherwise, Claire slipped underneath Chief Duke's arm, leaving him to issue his warnings from behind her.

"It could have facial recognition and any number of ways to identify us."

"I will have to agree," Agent Stevens tersely stated as he brought up the rear, "but I will also note that the science of secretive observation has no doubt increased to such a degree that if we were going to be spotted, we could have been done so by one of those holographic billboards or some mechanical bird up in the trees. Just keep an eye out, though I doubt we have yet to worry about anything in a place so public."

Ben and Lou almost beat Claire to the kiosk, but weren't quite in time to prevent her from looking it over. Essentially it looked like a simple flat-screen monitor on a stand hooded by a metal umbrella just wide enough for a couple of people to stand under and not get wet in the event of rain. The rest clustered around behind them, though Agent Hessman once again noticed some people glancing in their direction with odd looks. Young people, a cluster of them in their odd apparel.

"Okay now," Claire puzzled, "how do you work? I don't see any of those keyboards."

Her comment was immediately answered by the appearance of a menu of options hovering in the air before her. Startled, she jumped back a foot, straight into Ben's arms, giving Agent Hessman the opportunity to slip past her and stand before the screen.

"Voice activated and probably touch-screen," he presumed. He cleared his throat and directed his commands to the screen. "Current events, local and international."

The screen immediately blanked, replaced by another phrase floating in the air before him: *"No chip implant detected. Access will be limited."* Then this too blanked out to be replaced by a list of headlines.

"Chip implant?" Ben wondered as he looked over the other's shoulder. "Like our locator chips?"

"No doubt a lot more sophisticated," Agent Hessman agreed. "Okay, let's see what we can discover."

He reached out to press one of the selections and was rewarded by a video of a vicious storm at sea. Meanwhile, Claire returned to her task of observing all the futuristic delights around them. Across the street she saw a cluster of young people more conservatively dressed than others their age, with the studious look of college students. They all seemed to be looking back at them, so Claire did what came natural. She smiled pleasantly, fixed her hat more firmly against a sudden breeze, and kept looking around, while Agent Hessman kept at the kiosk, trying to find something useful.

That's when one young man in particular grew wide-eyed and nearly leapt across the street, nearly before the lights changed permitting pedestrians across.

"Oh my God," he called out as he came running over, "you *are* her."

Even Agent Hessman was distracted by the unexplained outburst, though not as much as Claire when the young man practically bowed before her as he introduced himself.

"I am *such* a fan."

"Somehow I really doubt that," she uncertainly replied, "but you are . . . ?"

"Oh, I'm sorry. My name is Jeffery Nezsmith, American exchange student. May I say what a great honor it is to meet you, Miss Hill. I never thought I'd have the honor of bumping into you."

"Yeah, uh . . . me neither."

To her shocked look no one else on the team had any ready answers.

10

FUTURE REPORTER

Jeffery Nezsmith grabbed Claire's hand and immediately began shaking it vigorously. Then, seeing the uncertain expression on her face, he dropped it with a quick apology.

"I'm sorry, but I'm just so flustered to meet you. As a history major of course I'd know you on sight. I remember the first story of yours I read was about your trip back to the Revolutionary War. You *really* made it come alive for me. That's what made me decide on history. And your story from the eighteen nineties when you nearly met your mother before you were born? Informative *and* comedic!"

"Uh," Claire began uncertainly, "you're welcome?"

"And this must be the rest of the team," the young man continued, going over first to Ben. "You must be *Mister* Hill—uh, Professor Ben Stein."

He reached out to take Ben's hand in a quick shake, during which Ben cast a quizzical glance at Agent Hessman. Lou replied with a shrug that might have said, "Go with it."

"How's it feel to be married to such a famed reporter, Professor Stein? Oh, and that looks like Captain Beck before he finally retired," the young man continued, breaking off from Ben to move on to the next one on the team. "I don't recognize the guy in the suit and sunglasses, but the big one must be the bodyguard of the day. Is this your first trip with Miss Hill?"

Chief Duke simply growled, to which the lad backed quickly away and continued his search of the team.

"I don't see Dr. Weiss with you, but he was never on all of them. But where's Agent Harris? Why isn't she with you? She *was* maid of honor at your wedding, after all."

"She's, uh, recovering," Claire replied.

"Oh, that's right," the young man said with a slap to his own forehead. "The 1919 incident where they first picked you up. Say, does this mean that this is your *first* trip out? Oh, I'm so thrilled!"

"Lou," Ben said, stepping up next to the government agent, "I think I'm starting to get the gist of things here."

"And I have an uncomfortable feeling that we're both getting the same gist. Uh, Mr. Nezsmith was it?"

"Just call me Jeffery."

"If you could give us the thumbnail of what you've heard of Miss Hill."

"Still calling her 'Miss Hill'—that should have been my *first* clue."

Claire broke in with a pleasant smile, taking the lead. "What he means is, this being my first trip to this particular time period, if you could just give me a little background of what you know about me so I can get an idea of where in my own timeline I happen to find myself."

"Of course!" Jeffery beamed. "As much traveling about as you do you always need to see when you are, make sure you're not getting ahead of yourself. Okay then."

Glancing around, he led them away from the corner, a few yards in the direction of the river. That's when they noticed a few details about the man with the sandy blond hair. Like the fact that he didn't look much older than Claire, and under one arm he was holding tight to what looked like some sort of laptop computer. Claire, meanwhile, came up next to Agent Hessman for a quick word.

"We can take advantage of this, Lou. We need a local, just like you guys needed me back in 1919. And it's not like we'd be messing up the past or anything, and he really does seem eager."

"Very well, Miss Hill, but only him. We don't need anyone else knowing about us; we're not supposed to be here, remember."

"Got it. You're a doll."

She gave him a quick peck on the cheek, then spun around to confront her new fan as they came to a stop under the eaves of the corner building. It looked like some sort of drugstore, its holographic sign billing it as the most reliable source of pill-form liver cancer cures.

"Okay, first," she began, "how exactly do you know of me?"

"Simple," Jeffery said. "You're just about the most famous cross-temporal reporter of all time. In certain circles, at least."

"Like history majors?"

"Yeah," he shyly admitted, "and temporal physics students, of course. I think I've read all the reports you ever wrote of your trips. Civil War, Watts Riot, a couple of back-to-back trips to the early eighteen hundreds, that trip to old China where Dr. Weiss's knowledge of physics got you guys a visit to the Imperial Court because they thought he was a traveling wizard —all of them."

"Uh, Miss Hill, if I may interject," Agent Hessman began, "but that report that you wrote of your experiences when we found you?"

"All filed away the way you told me to. No one outside the base has seen it."

"Oh, all her papers were under tight security for a while," Jeffery filled in, "but eventually a couple got to circulating, and after about fifty years the government finally released them. Now they're required reading for history and journalism majors."

To this Claire beamed a very broad smile to Ben, who rolled his eyes in response, followed by Claire giving a pleading shrug, then Ben pantomiming his defeat.

Agent Stevens finally spoke up. "This Mr. Nezsmith knows too much of our mission. We should do something to silence him."

"Oh, don't worry, I won't say a thing," Jeffery assured him. "I know all the rules of cross-temporal interaction." He then gave the man a closer look followed by a frown. "Poor replacement for Agent Harris. I was really hoping to meet her as well. Oh well."

"Uh, Jeffery," Claire began, "we could really use your help right now. You see, we're new to this time and could really use—"

"Oh my God, you want *me* to be your local! I wonder if that means I'm in one of your papers that I haven't read yet. No, of course not. Any reports on future travel would have been a lot more strictly quarantined. But sure, I'll do anything to help you out. What do you need?"

"To be blunt," Agent Hessman began, "we're looking for some Russian time travelers who kidnapped a friend of ours."

"Oh, the Time Bubble. It's down there at the university." He pointed down the street straight in the direction of the University of London, specifically at the large domed structure that Ben had said was new. "It's part of the History Department and usage is strictly overseen. Historical observations only allowed."

"And any Russians?" Claire pleasantly prompted.

"Well . . . I *did* hear that some Russian group has some time on it right now."

Hearing this, Agent Hessman pulled out his portable tracker and aimed it in the direction of the university. "Nothing," he announced. "We should be well within range, but no chip signal. They've moved her."

"No way you could have gotten in anyway," Jeffery told them. "Security is really tight over there."

Agent Hessman put his detector away, setting his mouth into a thin line. "That means our trail is cold. We have no way of knowing where they may have taken her, even if this was our own time. Mr. Nezsmith," he said, turning to the young man, "we're really going to need your help, but I should warn you: it's going to be dangerous."

The eager grin on the young man's face only got wider.

II

WARMING TRAIL

"**P**erhaps we should take this to a venue where a bunch of people just standing around looking suspicious won't stand out quite as much," Captain Beck suggested.

"Robert's right," Agent Hessman agreed. "Mr. Nezsmith, would you know of such a place?"

"Not too far from here," Jeffery replied. "This way."

Jeffery Nezsmith led the way, Chief Duke just behind him to act as human plowshare through the crowd for the others, with Agent Stevens bringing up the rear. Across the one busy street, down a block, then up a side street, during which time Agent Hessman took the opportunity to engage the college student in a little informative conversation, while Clair continued to look around at all the wonder about her and sigh by Ben's side.

"London is one of those places I wanted to go once I became a famous reporter," she remarked as they walked. "You know, out on assignment in the likes of London, Paris, Berlin, or Rome."

"Well, now you're here." Ben grinned. "Just a little later than you'd planned."

"I also wanted to treat my parents to a trip," she added. "Now I'll never . . . I wonder if they ever made it on their own."

"Feeling a bit melancholy?"

"That"—she sighed again—"and more than a little bit in shock, first from the wonders of your modern age and now this."

"The term is 'future shock,'" Ben supplied. "A term based on an old book someone wrote in the seventies about what life would be like in the futuristic nineties."

"Well, I'm suffering from plenty of future shock, I guess." She wrapped her right hand around his waist and pulled herself in closer to his side. "Fortunately, I have a fantastic shock-buffer," she added with a smile.

While Claire was noting the wonders by Ben's side, Agent Hessman was using the walk to grill Jeffery for a little information.

"The brief time I was on that kiosk, it showed a video of a storm at sea."

"Yeah, we get plenty of them," the college student admitted.

"This one seemed particularly vicious and perhaps a little unseasonal."

They passed up a string of small shops, each with its small holographic signage displaying its services. Shoes made on-site by robotic hands, an Indian restaurant boasting of a live human cook, an 'Auto-Seamstress,' another hatter, and perhaps the first bookstore with actual physical books they had yet seen in this century and a pretty rare sight even in their own.

Jeffery thought for a moment on Agent Hessman's words before replying with a shrug, "Yeah, I imagine they would seem pretty vicious compared to what you're used to."

"And the dikes," the agent also noted. "Since when does the river Thames have dikes like Holland?"

"Well, I'd say since about the last forty or fifty years, actually. It gets pretty wet and cold around here under the best of circumstances, though I'm just glad I'm not back home right now. I hear it's hurricane season again in the Midwest. An F six just ran through the middle of Kansas last week."

"F *six*? What manner of—"

"There we are," Jeffery suddenly indicated. "Park up ahead. Just in time, too, 'cause that sky looks like it's going to break wide-open any minute now."

He quickened his pace, the others following his example, while a glance up showed the reason for his concern. The clouds were dark gray and rapidly getting darker, the air temperature dropping by the second. The park that Jeffery had indicated stretched on for about a city block; a miniature landscape of rolling hills, quaint footbridges over little streams, a scattering of trees, and of course the occasional statues, though in this case not ones made of stone and mortar. As they stepped onto the grass they could see what at first looked like a statue of a warrior of many ages past standing proud with his brass spear; then a flicker and the statue shifted position, bearing his lance level as if before an enemy. The figure's proud features shifted to something more threatening and he stabbed the lance forward before flowing back to his previous noble stance.

Jeffery saw the look on Agent Hessman's face, not to mention everyone else's, and grinned. Claire in particular was hugging herself extra tightly to Ben's side.

"Holographic statues," the college student supplied. "Look pretty real, don't they? At least until you know how to spot the scan lines. This one's supposed to be of a figure out of Celtic mythology, but I remember one time when a few kids from the computer department at the university hacked the system and as a prank had it displaying a naked nymph from Greek mythology trying to seduce passersby. They got suspended for a week, and I got myself some great snapshots downloaded."

Across the small park he led them, right up to what looked like a park bench and accompanying overhang just as thunder rumbled from the sky and the first cold droplets began to come down. The bench was plastic and looked sculpted after an ocean wave, with no back, and long enough to seat four. The overhang stretched an extra couple of feet past either end and three extra feet each to the front and back; it looked like a flat blue plane curved down at the edges and raised along the center. It was just big enough to shelter them all as the skies opened up.

Agent Hill, Jeffery and Ben

Jeffery sat down in the middle of the bench, Agent Hessman to one side, Ben and Claire to the other, while Captain Beck stood behind them and Chief Duke took front position with a sharp eye out at their surroundings and anyone passing by. Agent Stevens stood off to one side just beneath the shelter, though he seemed to have an eye out for the underside of the roof just above them.

They watched as Jeffery put his case on his lap and opened it up. It was indeed a laptop, but the screen and a number of virtual controls floated in the air above its surface. In place of mechanical buttons there was a black panel, featureless until Jeffery activated his system; then the panel partitioned itself off into rows of buttons, complete with beveled surfaces rising up. Hovering in the air, starting an inch above the surface of the laptop and going up to fourteen inches above it, was the screen, filled now with a starry three-dimensional background and what looked like a row of winged toasters. Toasters flying through space shooting slices of toasted bread at each other.

Jeffery saw the looks on their faces and grinned sheepishly.

"My screen blanker. Based on the old toaster screen-blankers from back around your day."

A pass of his hand through the image and it vanished, replaced by a series of charts, rows of floating three-dimensional icons, and an open text field. Jeffery stabbed a finger into the text field, and it vanished in a flicker.

"Term paper," he explained.

"So *this* is what computer laptops are like nowadays," Ben said, while sitting beside him Claire was speechless with wonder.

"Not exactly top-of-the-line," Jeffery replied with a hint of pride, "but it's mine. Latest in holographics, high multitasking capability, all the usual hookups, including a built-in 3D printer for small stuff, Net access—the whole bit."

"And this is how you access the internet?" Agent Hessman now asked. "Because I noticed at that kiosk it said something about no chip implant being detected."

"Nearly everyone has a Net-chip implant, of course," Jeffery answered, "myself included. And it's great for general info access and stuff, but for really big assignments the bandwidth can be limited, at least not without giving someone an aneurism. So, that's when you break out a datapad. I need mine for my assignments, not to mention the latest in 3D games. Have you *seen* Car Wars 2550 in multiplexing 5200 p with a stag-core engine?"

The collective reply he received was a circle of blank faces, save from Chief Duke, who was still on guard detail, and Agent Stevens, who was examining one of the two poles that held up their protection against the weather. Meanwhile, just outside their shelter, the rain was coming down in sheets and the wind was tossing it all about —though somehow none of it seemed to get anything beneath the roof wet.

"No, I don't suppose you would have." Jeffery sighed. "Okay, to work. What do you need from me?"

"The Russians," Ben supplied. "We need to find them."

"And rescue poor Samantha," Claire added. "But how do we do that in a city *this* big?"

"A problem for which Mr. Nezsmith may have already given us an answer," Agent Hessman stated.

"I have?" The lad perked up. "Yay me. What'd I do?"

The pounding of the rain washed out nearly all sight and sound of the world without, the howling wind pushing it into a hard slant while chilling travelers to the bone. And yet, as Captain Beck now noticed, they all remained bone-dry and pleasantly warm.

"You said that nearly everyone has these chip implants," Agent Hessman said.

"Pretty much," Jeffery replied. "It's like a rite of passage when you hit thirteen."

"Including people from Russia?"

Jeffery's was not the only face to begin to brighten as Agent Hessman continued with his idea.

"Assuming the Russians did use the London time chamber to kidnap Samantha, then their chips would have been used at some point—"

"And could be tracked!" Jeffery completed. "You know, as a history major I have access to the facility, and with a little help from a computer-major friend of mine, I might be able to log in to the system and get the chip codes of the last few users. If they're Russians, then we have your guys."

"Do you think your friend would do it?" Claire asked.

"And without revealing anything about us," Agent Hessman added.

"My friend's a conspiracy nut," Jeffery said. "All I have to do is tell her that I may have a lead on some new conspiracy and that I need the info. Not a problem. Just give me a few minutes."

"Then before you do," Captain Beck broke in, "could you explain one thing to me?"

With a pass of his hand toward the wall of water just behind him, he cast the young man a questioning look.

"Just a flash storm. Give it a few minutes and it'll be back to London sunshine again, which is to say weak and fog-filtered."

"Not that," Captain Beck amended, "but the fact that the slant of the rain should be drenching all of us and Claire's floppy sunhat should be a drooping mess by now."

"Oh, you mean the rain field?" Jeffery replied. "Just a low-intensity force field designed to work specifically against free water. That's why I headed us for one of the sheltered benches. Okay, time to contact my friend."

He then placed a palm onto the flat surface of his laptop and fixed his gaze on something far away.

"A rain field," Claire marveled. "That is just so . . . Wow."

"Quite remarkable," Ben admitted. "But, Lou, you don't seem too impressed."

"We're a hundred years in the future," the agent replied. "I expect the fantastic. What has me more concerned is why Agent Stevens there has found such intimate interest in the structure of our shelter. Stevens?"

Stevens paused his examination of their shelter, which currently included having a palm pressed against the ocean-blue plastic-looking pole sweeping down to the ground from his side of the roof, and replied in an efficient tone: "I felt a slight prickling in the outer housing of this structure, which could be from this protective field just mentioned, but I may have discovered other possibilities."

"Such as?" Agent Hessman prompted.

Agent Stevens pointed a finger to a spot on the overhang's ceiling just above them. At first all anyone could see was more of the blue ocean-wave pattern sweeping across the surface, but then Agent Hessman narrowed his eyes and stood atop the bench for a closer look. Agent Stevens was pointing to a single blue dot.

"A blue dot," he noted.

"It looks like it was painted as part of the ocean spray," Claire remarked. "Or maybe a stray droplet of paint."

"In a place as computer-exact as everything around here appears to be," Agent Stevens replied, "I would rule that out and say it's likely that it may be some form of observation device. Like a highly miniaturized camera."

"That's sounding a bit paranoid," Ben remarked.

"I get paid to be paranoid," Agent Stevens blandly stated.

Agent Hessman took another closer look, then got down off the bench with a curt nod. "I will err on the side of paranoia. We need to move as soon as the weather permits us. Chief Duke, have you spotted anything?" he said.

The large man was peering out into the sheets of rain, but in a far more specific direction than he had been before. He replied with a slight nod and said, "Hard to make out exactly through all this rain, but it looks like some local cops in some very unusual uniforms. It looks like they're going from shelter to shelter."

"Then I'm not taking any chances. Mr. Nezsmith, if you would kindly come out of your trance."

He reached down a hand to gently touch the college student's shoulder. Nothing happened at first; then Jeffery's eyes blinked. Meanwhile, the weather outside changed as suddenly as it had begun, the rain suddenly slacking off as the clouds quickly began to clear. By the time

Jeffery was back with them, it was sunny once again and the wind had dropped completely away.

"See?" he said, glancing around. "I told you the rain would stop. Oh, my friend's ready to help. I had to tell her this convoluted story that may have suggested a conspiracy from the future; I just never mentioned *whose* future. She's a comp-sci major, but her father also got her interested in—"

Agent Hessman dropped a hand onto the lad's head and turned it a few degrees until Jeffery's gaze was directed across the park to where the uniformed men were looking around. Blue-and-green uniforms with a symbol on their chests that looked like three concentric rings around a capital *T*. Immediately he stopped his chattering and his eyes widened.

"Time cops."

"They're really called 'time cops'?" Ben pondered. "Nothing more inventive, or something that reduces to a cool acronym?"

"They've picked up your time trace," Jeffery quickly explained, immediately slapping closed his laptop. "They want to send you back before you see any more of the future."

"Not before we rescue Samantha," Agent Hessman firmly decided. "We need to find a new place for you to work your hack."

"Oh," Jeffery said, getting to his feet with the rest, "I'm still connected to my friend." A tap of an index finger to the side of his head and he grinned. "I'm chipped, remember. Always connected."

"Then you can work on this hack while on the run?" Agent Hessman asked.

"Of course."

"Then start running."

The men in the unusual uniforms looked up from their current inquiry and across the park at the next nearest inhabited shelter-bench— which happened to be the team's own. They saw a group of people starting to hurriedly leave and immediately broke into pursuit.

12

TRACE AND CHASE

gent Hessman saw the way the uniformed men were looking in their direction and wasted no time with pretense. He broke into a run, Chief Duke now taking on the role of bulldozer as they charged across the park. Behind them the uniforms broke into a run as well, and the chase was on.

Over one small rolling hill, over a footbridge, then nearly colliding with a park statue. Chief Duke had one arm in front and thought perhaps to bowl it over until he discovered that it was another holographic statue. He charged right into a centaur drawing back his bow, to come out the other side just as the arrow was launched into nothingness. One by one the others in turn leaped through or around the projection, Claire passing by just as it changed from a centaur to a satyr playing his reed pipes.

"I'm not sure," she said, "but I think that satyr was getting fresh with me."

The far side of the park ended at a busy street running along its edge. Behind them they could see the group of uniforms spreading out as they raced after them, while the one in the center had taken something out of his vest pocket and was talking into it.

"They're trying to outflank us," Agent Hessman said, "which means one direction left. Straight ahead."

Ben glanced up, looking around for some sort of intersection or crossing, but saw none. "No place to cross," he called back as they all continued to run.

"Like I said, *straight* across."

"And if we get hit?" Claire asked.

"I'm betting that won't be a problem. Now *move* it."

Chief Duke was the first to leap across the street, heedless of any oncoming traffic. Behind him raced Agent Hessman and Ben, followed by Claire, then Captain Beck huffing and puffing, and finally Agent Stevens. Agent Stevens fished something out from a pocket and tossed it behind him before picking up his speed and making a point of not looking back again.

The brilliant flash of light that came from what Agent Stevens had thrown in the way of their pursuers was accompanied by several sets of brakes screeching. A row of cars suddenly came to a halt before their drivers were even aware of a problem. One bumper missed Chief Duke by inches, another giving Captain Beck sudden concern with its nearness. Claire ran with one hand holding down her hat and an apologetic smile for the motorists she passed by, including one elderly man who gasped in recognition of her face, then gave her a two-fingered salute off the top of his head. As they reached the other side Ben noticed that several of the cars looked to have no drivers at all.

Chief Duke led them straight into the nearest alley, shoving one slow pedestrian out of the way with a quickly muttered, "Sorry, sir." As they all barreled in after him, Ben shot a question to Agent Hessman: "Lou, how'd you know?"

"They're experimenting with self-driving cars in *our* century," came the reply. "I simply decided it would be a good bet that all cars now have some form of automatic reactions against hitting things. Nezsmith, we need to lose them."

Jeffery was in a half trance, aware enough to keep running along with the rest, but not entirely focused on much else. When he heard his name, though, he blinked once and called out a reply: "Uh, this alley turns left up ahead and goes into a sort of back-alley mall. Exit at the far side. Hopefully, the alley will be too narrow for the remotes to follow us in."

A glance up by Agent Hessman gave him an idea of what Jeffery was talking about. Another one of those three-foot miniature delivery drones they'd seen earlier, only this one had nothing to deliver and seemed to be trying to find a wide enough way down.

"Good enough. Chief Duke, a straight line. Agent Stevens, we need a new obstacle course behind us."

"Sue wouldn't have needed that big flash of light," Claire whispered discreetly to Ben. "She would have found a way to take them all out herself."

"And I should have an answer for you shortly," Jeffery answered.

Chief Duke said nothing in reply to his command, simply acted. As the alley came to its left turn at the end, he shouted ahead to the clusters of people passing by, "One side. We're in a hurry!"

At their rear, Agent Stevens tossed out a couple more balls. When the first small business they came to was a little café with outdoor tables for two, he turned one over and tossed it behind them, then another while still running.

To their left was what looked like some Net café; then ahead on their right, a small music shop that appeared to be dedicated to very small stringed instruments, an antique store, and a very low-key entrance down a set of stairs to a place the hovering holographic signage above identified as Alley Nights. A curio shop farther ahead on the left, labeled Through the Looking Glass, displayed an assortment of goodies in the window themed after white rabbits and curious creatures. At the end on the right was what another floating sign made out to be Harm's Cinephile.

The architecture throughout remained classic old London, accented of course by the hovering holographic signs and the occasional window display mixing a combination of robotics and holography, such as the Through the Looking Glass shop that had a girl in a white dress continually chasing a rabbit across the window display to a backdrop of varying scenes from the books.

In their wake came a flash of light and sound from the first of the flash-bangs that Agent Stevens had left, then two more as their pursuers ran afoul of them. A response came in the form of a couple of shots whizzing past their ears. None of them hit, though, thanks to the disruptive flashes of light.

"I'd still feel safer if that was Sue picking up our rear," Claire remarked as they ran. "Though I must say that, for a converted alley, this place is pretty clean. I don't see one speck of trash anywhere."

"That's the bugs," Jeffery replied, "same thing as cleaned up the oceans."

"The what?"

"The plastic-eating bugs. Invented by some old guy from Caltech named Dillon Marshal."

Claire beamed. "Well, that sounds like a very good use of bugs."

"Enough talk, and through there," Agent Hessman said, pointing to Harm's Cinephile. "Looks like a theater."

Behind them the sound of electrified gunfire was accompanied by a crash and a curse as a blinded pursuer fell victim to one of Agent Stevens's overturned tables. As they ducked through the entrance, they were greeted by what at first looked like a pimply-faced teen in a red-and-white concession uniform, until they saw the robotic features and the fact that his waist ended on a metal post.

"Tickets please."

"The kid's paying," Chief Duke growled on his way past.

"Thank you for selecting Harm's Cinephile, delivering you the best of today's holographic upgrades to yesteryear's old movie classics. Today's feature is *Midway*, starring . . ."

Agent Hessman ignored the spiel as he pushed on through, as did Ben and Claire, though Claire paused briefly to marvel at the detail of the faux-human face until Captain Beck urged her through. When Jeffery was passing through the old-style turnstile, he simply glanced over at the robot, who replied with a nod of its head and cutting off its presentation.

"Thank you for your purchase," the robot-greeter stated. "A row of seats in continuous succession sufficient for your party has been reserved."

The lobby ahead of them had a concession stand of a type common to theaters before Ben or Lou might have been born, complete with popcorn maker, and all manned by another smiling robot on a stick.

"They try to mimic the old theater-going experience of about a hundred and fifty years back as much as they can," Jeffery briefly explained as they headed across the room, "which in some places includes sticky floors and a noisy robotic patron in the rear of the theater."

They spotted a curtained-off entry, ignored the pleas of the concession-bot as to what manner of popcorn they might like, and hurried across to the curtain as Agent Hessman called to Jeffery, "How's the hack?"

"Just confirmed that Russia had the place rented out and recently used it, but not much else. We have their chip IDs, though, and are starting a worldwide trace."

"Good. Stay on it."

They entered what at first looked less like a theater and more like a World War II war zone, complete with shells screaming through the air, bombs exploding, gunfire everywhere, and sweaty, grimy men charging at one another. Claire gave a sharp yelp and leaped into Ben's arms, who himself was looking for somewhere to run to. Chief Duke started swinging a fist at the nearest approaching soldier, and Captain Beck reached for something in his pants pocket that looked roughly pistol shaped, while Agent Stevens slipped into a martial arts stance. Agent Hessman, however, remained calm and carefully eyed the situation for details.

Such as the rows of heads sticking up above the seats the people were seated in as they all quietly took it in.

"Hey, I haven't seen this one in ages," Jeffery whispered as he calmly walked down the beach, or, as the rest now began to perceive it, the aisle.

"You mean, this is only a movie?" Claire hesitantly asked.

"One we're not staying to watch," Agent Hessman told them. "Chief Duke, find us a rear exit. I've no doubt our pursuers have other ways of still tracking us."

As the battle raged on around them, it seemed as if they could hear some fresh voices back in the lobby. This only quickened their pace until they found the exit sign and hurriedly left the theater.

They came back out into daylight and a small alley just off a busy street. A few steps later they were quickly making their way into the crowds, trying to become one with them.

"Got it!" Jeffery enthusiastically announced.

"The trace?" Ben asked.

"Found them through their gamer tags," Jeffery explained as they picked up their pace. "One of them is a player on GOW."

"Huh?" Captain Beck remarked.

"What's a 'gow'?" Ben asked.

"What's a gamer tag?" Claire asked.

"GOW," Jeffery eagerly explained, "stands for Galaxy of War and is *the* most popular game on the planet. It currently has over a billion players involved. Why, at last update, just the number of options alone—"

"We get it," Agent Hessman cut him off, "you have their location. Now let's get off someone's radar long enough to make use of that fact."

"I'll see if I can get my friend to do something about putting off the tracker network a bit," Jeffery offered. "In the meantime, just head for someplace with a lot of signal traffic; that always confuses the system. Uh, plenty of people and lots of animated signs. A lot of people are getting off work and school, which means many of them will be logging on to GOW, so any large crowd—"

"We get it, lots of signal traffic," Agent Hessman stated. "Chief Duke . . . ?"

To the unspoken question, Chief Duke pointed ahead of them. They were coming to an intersection that was crowded with not only people but a small herd of little cafés, all of which were filled with young people.

"Perfect. Everyone, pick it up but try not to look like we're running. First crowded café we come to in the middle of that and we'll stop to assess our options."

While Chief Duke led the way toward what looked to be a particularly crowded café, Agent Stevens was glancing over his shoulders in search of any pursuers. They were about a block away from the alley they had left, with a crowd of people between them and it, when Agent Stevens's sharp eyes caught sight of a couple of the same uniformed men as before emerging. They paused at the edge of the alley, one of them taking out a handheld device to briefly consult it before heading off across the street and away from the group.

"We lost them for now," Agent Stevens reported in a low tone.

"Good," Claire said with a sigh, at last bringing her hand down from its place in keeping her hat from blowing away, "because I did not come dressed for another chase. We had a few of them back in 1919. Jeffery, you're my biggest fan. Do *all* my trips involve chases like this?"

"*Do* they," the young man eagerly replied. "Why, they've made some of the most exciting ones into 3D movies. My favorite is this—"

"Enough," Agent Hessman cut in. "Time to look inconspicuous. People, I hope you like Persian food."

He led the way into what lay immediately ahead of them: a bright yellow storefront with equally bright holographic signage proclaiming both its Persian specialties and the claim "Now in Our Hundredth Year!"

13

SABOTAGE ATTEMPT

Back in the year 2020 the clock was just hitting 10:30 p.m. in the hidden New Mexico base when Agent Harris and Dr. Weiss came hobbling out of the infirmary, with respective canes, Agent Harris's pace looking a little uncertain at first.

"Maybe you should wait a bit longer before trying to walk, Sue," Dr. Weiss was saying. "It's only been a few hours."

"Which is a few hours too long of just laying on my ass," she replied. "I can out-hobble you any day of the week."

"Then may I challenge you to a cane race? First one to the end of the hall springs for the next pudding cup at the cafeteria. The workout should be good for you."

Sue grinned, then started hobbling along faster. "Just remember I like my banana pudding," she said.

And so, watched by a nurse peeking out from the ER and a couple of passing soldiers making way for them, the pair started a cane race toward the end of the hall, where it joined up with another one perpendicular to it. At first Dr. Weiss took the lead with his stately, dignified walk, but a determined Agent Harris powered through any lingering weaknesses she may have been suffering and set herself into a fast-paced hobble that had her pulling ahead of Dr. Weiss.

"That dignified walk of yours is going to get you a distant second." She grinned.

"A gentleman never corrects a lady, but in this case . . . not if I can help it."

Sue was a full three feet in front and nearly to the end of the hall when something literally appeared in a twinkle of prismatic lights at the intersection ahead. Three men that Dr. Weiss immediately recognized and to which the nearest soldiers instantly reacted.

"Those are the same three as before," Dr. Weiss gasped. "Where did you take my niece, you Russian thugs?" He raised his cane, trying to wave it about threateningly.

Agent Harris immediately sized up the situation and changed her course into a half tackle of her friend, bowling Dr. Weiss off to the side and against a wall, then down to the floor. "Stay down," she ordered. Turning around as quickly as her condition would allow, she glanced over to see what was going on.

Three soldiers already lay on the ground twitching, each one having fallen victim to the electrified bullets, while three more were charging down from the other hall with pistols aimed and shouting threats for the Russians' surrender.

Agent Harris flattened herself against the wall and started creeping her way closer to the intersection. The soldiers fired their guns only to see their bullets be deflected once a foot away from the Russians, followed by the Russians then getting off their return fire. Three more soldiers quickly joined the others napping on the ground.

One of the Russians called out to the other two while taking out a small palm-sized device for a quick glance at its display. Agent Harris tapped a finger to her right ear and the small device hidden within it and whispered, "Harris here. If my Russian's not too rusty, these guys are here to sabotage the time chamber and shut it down. I'll do what I can up here."

Message sent, she removed her finger and crept around the corner and positioned herself against the wall, with one hand gripping tightly the head of her cane. A moment later the central Russian snapped another order and they spun around and jogged directly past Agent Harris's position. They took no notice of the invalid with the cane, judging her as obviously harmless, and Agent Harris did her best to look weak and helpless, at least until they were about halfway past her, at which point her cane suddenly whipped out into a swift arc that took the middle one to her left behind the knee on its way up to the back of the head of the one just to her right. The left one fell back into the third behind him, while the right one bowled over to hit the ground unconscious. Agent Harris turned slower than her normal but still fast enough to face the one on the ground just as he was getting to his feet, while his companion behind him was also getting back up and getting a few feet of distance from the encounter.

Agent Harris's cane smacked the rising figure straight in the center of his forehead like a pool stick hitting a cue ball. This time when the man fell back he did not stir. This left the third one at the back to face Agent Harris alone, who suddenly did not seem quite as helpless as her cane and condition might imply. The remaining Russian eyed who it was that was facing him, then suddenly widened his eyes a bit in alarm and quickly brought up his pistol.

"Agent Susan Harris," he said in thickly accented English.

She was leaning against her cane, obviously still recovering from her experience in time travel, yet her face was set with determination, while the one conscious Russian found that his hand gripping his pistol was shaking a little. Then he found that his hand had gone suddenly numb, and his pistol dropped to his feet from brief contact with Agent Harris's cane. She had stepped one foot forward, swung her cane round, and, before her body could sway too much to one side or the other, smashed the end of her cane down hard across the other's hand, bringing her cane back into place in time to catch herself.

A few choice words escaped the Russian's lips, none of which can be translated in polite company. Then, with his good hand, he quickly reached into a pocket and drew out a round disk. More soldiers were just racing down the hall.

"I did not sign up to face *you*, Agent Harris."

A press of his disc and he, his two companions lying unconscious, and even his fallen pistol shimmered in rainbow flickers and vanished before all eyes.

"Coward," Agent Harris muttered under her breath. "Can't even face an invalid with a cane."

While the new guards came in to examine the six fallen victims of the futuristic bullets and scour the area for anything that might have been left behind, Sue hobbled back around the corner to where she had left Dr. Weiss. He was midway to his feet, still struggling with his cane, when her free hand reached out to help him the rest of the way up.

"Are you all right, Sam? Sorry I had to shove you away like that, but the way they were going with those guns of theirs, you might have gotten hurt."

"Why, thank you, Sue." Then, once fully on his feet with cane in place, he turned the subject around. "But what about *you*? You could have landed back in the infirmary again. You should not have been fighting them in your condition."

"What fight? This may be my first encounter with these guys, but these future Russians seem to rely too much on their high-tech widgets and neglect good old-fashioned training. Pathetic, really. They should be embarrassed."

"That one looked more terrified," Dr. Weiss said with a little grin. "It looked like he recognized you, and not for the better I might add."

"I guess I have a reputation in the future," she said with a shrug. "Now let's head back. We still have a cane race to finish."

She started off once again in her cane-assisted hobble, tossing one last comment over her shoulder as she went.

"And you were right: the workout *was* good for me."

Dr. Weiss replied with a chuckle and then hobbled along after her.

14

TIME TO THINK

In the London of the future, the group was seated in a corner of the Persian deli and café, a small cluster of tables to themselves, while the rest of the crowded café was festooned with groups of chatting college students, the occasional college professor, and others just off work coming in for a quick bite to eat or a relaxing drink. Every table had a flat screen built onto its surface, above which projected various displays, though most seemed filled with views of space and charging vessels of one fanciful design or another.

"They're all playing GOW," Jeffery assured them. "Don't worry, no one'll notice anything we say or do. And my friend tells me that our trackers have been put off the scent for a while."

"Good," Agent Hessman replied. "Now, according to my timepiece, it's eleven fifteen New Mexico time, and about . . ."

"Four fifteen London time," Jeffery supplied.

"Thank you, Mr. Nezsmith. I want to get this finished up as quickly as we can, and Samantha rescued. Now, I recall you saying something about finding our Russians."

"We traced their IDs to an orbital station," Jeffery supplied.

"*Orbital?*" Captain Beck remarked.

"As in up in space?" Claire asked. "How are we ever going to get up *there*?"

"We'll never get to them in time," Ben said with a shake of his head.

But just as hopes were starting to fall, Jeffery put in a suggestion with such nonchalance that the rest nearly missed it: "Just take the suborbital. Have you up there within the day."

"You say that like hopping up into space is an everyday occurrence," Agent Hessman said, eyeing him suspiciously.

"It is. Flights to orbit are pretty common nowadays. In fact, the station I traced the Russians to is a major tourist trap. Space Vegas. Been there a couple times myself . . . uh, for school projects, of course."

"*Space* Vegas?" Ben grinned.

"Yeah," Jeffery said. "It's like the original Las Vegas only . . . spacier."

"Okay, given that's a thing," Agent Hessman stated, "we still have no way of paying for a trip like that."

"It's not all *that* expensive," Jeffery told them. "The university maintains a private shuttle for students going up there for various projects, but we also use it for holiday breaks. I can use my school pass to get you guys up there."

"Why, that would be *great*!" Claire exclaimed. "Then we can rescue Samantha. Thank you *so* much!" She reached out and nearly smothered Jeffery in a tight hug, after which his response was midway between embarrassment and fan-boy gratitude.

"Claire Hill just hugged me. I'm not going to take a bath for a *week*."

"You're a college student. Why change things?" Captain Beck quipped with a grin.

"Hold on, let me check my expense account."

It took only a moment of Jeffery's entranced look for him to return with an answer.

"I have enough university credit for one or two of you, but I'll have to get some help for the rest."

"Do what you can, Mr. Nezsmith. It is imperative that we rescue our missing party as quickly as we can."

"I'll see if a few of my friends can help. Hold on."

While Jeffery once again went into his trance, the rest finally had time to consult with one another about what they had seen.

"So many questions," Ben remarked.

"See?" Claire told him. "This is how it feels every day for me."

"As much as the rules may say that we need to minimize our knowledge of the future," Agent Hessman told them all, "we need to get as much information as we can. We still do not know *why* they kidnapped Samantha. Any piece of information could be pertinent, so let's start spitballing. What are some of the things that you all have noticed?"

"Oh, so *many* things," Claire said, marveling. "Of course, I'm still not entirely sure what the rest of you would consider new and amazing. Those floating signs, the clean alleys, how ridiculously tall the buildings have gotten. And the cars: they make barely a sound, and yet I don't see any of that awful smoke coming from the back ends of them like back in 2020."

"They must be electric cars," Ben told her. "The only problem with electric cars in our own time was the batteries. The things weigh a ton and take up a lot of resources to make."

A flicker of his eyelids and Jeffery was back with them in time to catch the tail end of Claire's statement.

"Oh, you'd be surprised how small and cheap car batteries have become," he answered. "Once they found out how to do that everything came out electric."

"Okay, what else?" Agent Hessman prompted.

"The spy craft," Agent Stevens remarked. "As small as they can apparently make their equipment, I can think of a number of places where they could be placed."

"Weapons," Chief Duke put in. "They would be a lot better. Wouldn't mind getting my hands on some."

"Those walls along the Thames," Ben put in. "I was in London once, and they never had dikes there before. Nor was the weather quite so . . . unpredictable."

"Use to be worse," Jeffery casually remarked. "There was quite a bit of flooding before they got the dike system built, and the weather satellites work wonders to reduce the incidence of class-six hurricanes around the world. Not to mention the carbon-capture machines."

"I still like how clean some of the streets look," Claire remarked. "And the air smells so fresh and clean. Not like New York back in 2020."

A look at Claire and then to Jeffery as the college student suddenly began looking a little nervous, and Captain Beck put in his own observation on the matter: "I think our Miss Hill has once again brought attention to something crucial. My young man, I would like to hear more about how the environment was so miraculously cleaned up."

"Well, it's nothing spectacular, really, just the way things are now," Jeffery replied. "The weather may still be a little off-center, and they're still trying to figure out how much of that is due to sunspots or whatever, but the oceans are pristine and there's very little trash lying around on the ground."

"I realize much of that can be bundled under the general classification of 'progress,'" Ben said, "but how in the world did you manage to clear up the oceans?"

"Just the old plastic-eating bug. Once it was released, it went to work and cleaned it all up. Of course that *did* result in that global catastrophe. Here, I can show you a few videos of how the oceans look now. Pretty stormy, though, so it might be hard to tell the difference."

As Jeffery started to reach out to the screen at the center of their table, Hessman grabbed his arm and held it in place.

"I would rather hear about this 'global catastrophe' if you don't mind. What happened?"

The young man hesitated, glancing around at a small circle of eyes that suddenly were all focused rather intently on himself alone. Even Claire was looking at him less with her previous smile and more with the intense glare of a reporter on the trail of a fresh lead.

"I . . . really don't know how much I should tell you. The rules of cross-temporal interactions and all."

Agent Stevens looked as if he was ready to put the man under a spotlight and start grilling him, Chief Duke was balling up one fist suggestively, and Agent Hessman had the dispassionate stare of the robots they had been encountering. Claire's, though, was the hardest gaze to meet. She gazed at him first with a studied look, then broke out into a slight smile and pleasant voice.

"Oh, please tell us. It might make the difference in rescuing our friend."

"I, uh . . . Well, that is . . . Okay, but . . . Well, this guy named Dillon Marshal of Caltech came up with this bug that eats plastic; then they set it loose into the oceans. Oh, it did a great job of breaking down all sorts of plastics, even handling the microplastics. And for a while it worked. But then the bug escaped onto land and started wreaking havoc on plastics still in use. Even before that there were incidents in the oceans, though. Things like diving suits had just enough plastics in them to make breaking down while in a deep dive pretty fatal, or components in submarines and underwater structures. On land, though, we're talking everything from medical equipment to airplanes. Those planes would be sitting in their hangers and then, when being towed out to get ready for flight, would just fall apart."

"That sounds like a disaster," Claire gasped.

"Oh, it was, some fifty-odd years ago. Fortunately, once outside of the ocean the bug had a pretty limited range of environments in which it could survive."

"Hmmm." Agent Hessman was beginning to get a thoughtful look that Ben had come to recognize as meaning he was catching on to something. "Allow me to guess, Mr. Nezsmith: on land it can survive only where it is pretty cold."

"Cold and cloudy, yes," Jeffery replied, now a bit puzzled. "But how did you know?"

"Just continue, Mr. Nezsmith."

"Yes, well, anyway, while it wreaked havoc on the world in general, it was especially hard in a few places. Places like major parts of Canada, the Scandinavian countries, and"—he looked up at Agent Hessman with a look of wonder dawning across his face—"Russia. In fact, it was such a disaster for Russia that they were instantly reduced to third-world status.

Their industry, military equipment, the works got hit. Even after all this time they still haven't recovered."

"Russia," Agent Hessman repeated with a knowing nod. "Now we know how they fit into this. At least in part. What about the bug *now*?"

"Oh, they have new plastics that the bug won't eat; made them out of hemp, I think. And they have better ways of breaking them down once they're no longer in use."

"But from the sounds of it," Ben said, "Russia must have been left pretty devastated."

"They can barely find a couple of working planes to get off the ground," Jeffery sadly reported, "while the rest of the world has suborbital flights that can take you around the world in under an hour . . . Hey, I may have said too much. I'm really not sure how much of this you guys should know."

Claire reached out a hand to briefly hold one of his own as her soothing words touched his ears. "It's okay. You've told us enough, I'm sure."

To Claire's look Agent Hessman replied with a nod. Jeffery visibly sighed in relief; then the uncomfortable moment was suddenly interrupted as he went briefly back into his trance.

"Russia was left devastated," Captain Beck remarked. "So we know they're desperate, but for what? What does Miss Weiss have that they want?"

"Another piece of the puzzle we have yet to discover, Robert," Agent Hessman stated. "Once we have enough pieces, then we can unravel the rest."

Suddenly Jeffery perked up, all signs of his guilty look gone.

"Just heard back from my hacker friend. She managed to pool together enough university credits from her school chums to get passes for most of you, but two will have to stay behind. I'm sorry, but that's the best we can do."

"We'll just have to make sure that it's enough then, Mr. Nezsmith. Obviously, anyone staying behind on the ground would be in far too much danger by themselves doing nothing. "The possibilities," Agent

Stevens blandly began to recite, "would include being tracked down by the time cops, displaying undo lack of familiarity with current customs, running afoul of one problem or another due to the lack of a chip or other device, not to mention the possibilities of encountering hidden observation devices . . ."

As he was reciting, Jeffery bent forward for a quiet word with Claire.

"He really doesn't have any personality, does he?"

"Not really," Claire agreed.

"It's a pity that Agent Harris couldn't come with you on this trip. I'd have *loved* to meet her."

"You'd have liked her."

"She's a fan favorite in certain circles. Why, they even made a couple of vid-flicks about her. 'Agent Harris versus the Cyberdinos of 2424' was one of my favorites. Of course a lot of people may have gotten an exaggerated impression of her abilities, but I tend to stick right with the original source materials."

"My articles."

"Exactly!"

"The point *is*," Agent Hessman continued, "whoever we leave down on the ground will have to activate their beacons and return to our native time."

Agent Stevens again spoke up: "Then the choice is obvious: Miss Hill is not really a mission specialist, and Professor Stein's specialty lies in the past, not the future."

"What?" Claire instantly objected. "But it was *my* idea to—"

"I don't think you could have picked a worse choice," Captain Beck said with a shake of his head. "I'd volunteer myself before either of those two."

"No volunteering will be needed," Agent Hessman said. "I've already decided. Stevens and Chief Duke. Everyone else has mission-critical status."

"Understood, sir," Chief Duke said with a slight nod.

"You will be without your backup," Agent Stevens pointed out.

"The other option would be to be without some of our core mission personnel," Agent Hessman replied. "Captain Beck's duty is to make sure this mission sees success no matter what, and Miss Hill has proven her skills in the past."

"*Way* in the past," Claire said with a slight grin. "Sorry, couldn't resist."

"What we need now is a convenient alley," Agent Hessman stated. "Mr. Nezsmith, after your lead."

Jeffery looked once around at the sea of zombielike faces, shrugged, and then replied, "Here would be as good a place as any. Everyone's too involved with their GOW games, and the orders are taken and delivered by robotic means, so who's going to notice?"

Indeed, besides the customers, there was not a living worker that anyone could see. Orders were spoken at the tables and then delivered by wheeled carts that traveled from kitchen to table, and while the place must have had close to fifty customers in it, every one of them was fully engrossed in whatever scene lay at the other end of their chip implant.

"You would appear to be correct, Mr. Nezsmith. Chief Duke, Agent Stevens, please activate your beacons. When you arrive home update the general on the situation."

"Yes, sir," Chief Duke replied.

"Immediately, sir," Agent Stevens echoed.

Jeffery's attention was riveted as the pair took out their discs from within their jackets; then, standing up and stepping away from the table, each pressed the button at the center of his disc. A man-sized tornado of rainbow colors spun around the pair, and a moment later both had vanished.

"That is just so . . . ," Claire began. "Ben, what's a good modern word for that?"

"You could try 'cool,'" he suggested.

"Then that is just so *cool* to watch. Is that what we looked like when we vanished?"

"Okay, to business." Agent Hessman stood up, those remaining following his lead. He simply glanced at Jeffery, who took his cue.

Chief Duke Stephens

"Arranging passes out of Heathrow as we speak. Everything should be ready by the time we arrive."

"Good."

They walked out of the café, passing around oblivious diners. As they left through one of the front doors a voice came at them in a mock Persian accent wishing them a good day. Once outside and heading down the walkway, Agent Hessman pulled the college student up beside him for a few words.

"While I appreciate your friends' helping us out, I am concerned about the growing circle of people that know of our activity."

"Don't worry. I gave my friend a good cover story, and she knows enough to give each of her friends a completely different cover story. It'll be slick as ice."

"I'm still not sure," Agent Hessman told him.

"I'm with Lou," Captain Beck said, coming up behind them. "I can only imagine what sort of security measures they have around here."

"Just the usual," Jeffery said. "Video, audio, infrared, facial recognition hooked up to a global database, chemical detection—all in your standard thumbnail camera."

If Agent Hessman had any increased doubts from that litany, he was not showing them. The greater worry on his mind was the same as it was before: rescuing Samantha Weiss.

15

HEATHROW SPACEPORT

The trip to Heathrow Spaceport involved a trip on the Underground, which at this point in time had been replaced with something just a little faster. A fact they first noticed when they were suddenly slammed back in their seats after briefly wondering why train seats now looked more like miniature acceleration couches. Claire had barely gotten her seatbelt buckled in time, while beside her Ben had barely caught his breath in time. Once the acceleration eased up and the pressure against them lifted, Captain Beck was the first to offer a comment on the experience.

"What in the name of . . . ? If I had a heart condition, I don't think I'd have survived that."

"Never ridden on a bullet train before?" Jeffery asked.

"Is *that* what this is?"

"I rode the Underground when I was in London that one time," Ben put in, "and it wasn't a bullet train back then."

"Apparently another future upgrade," Agent Hessman calmly remarked. "How long before we arrive, Mr. Nezsmith?"

"Not long. Then there's the shuttle through the airport to where the flight takes off from. You should be up in orbit in about an hour. Then you can☐ — Wait a sec; priority all-points coming through."

This time when Jeffery briefly went into his trance, Claire cast a concerned look to Ben, who glanced to Lou, who in turn replied with a noncommittal look as he awaited what Jeffery had to say.

"Local police have a bulletin out for a group that sounds pretty much like you guys," Jeffery quietly stated a moment later.

"Another upgrade?" Ben asked with concern on his face. "They can not only track us but upload a wanted poster to everyone with a chip in their head?"

"Yes and no," Jeffery said after another briefer faraway look. "They have pictures, but they're only of the big guy and Mr. Robot Glasses."

"Duke and Stevens," Agent Hessman stated, "the ones we sent home."

"A close call," Captain Beck agreed. "But we'll have to be a lot more careful."

"It also means that their tech isn't perfect," Agent Hessman noted. "Beyond our understanding as to how it works, but still fallible."

"It might not be the technology that's fallible but the people operating it," Claire amended. "That's got to be true in *any* century."

"Miss Hill is right," Jeffery agreed. "For at least a good century, computer hackers have gotten into supposedly secure systems by hacking not just the tech but the people using them. My hacker friend's always going on about how social engineering plays a good role in a hacker's toolkit."

"Then that's what we go for from now on," Agent Hessman decided. "We can't beat their tech, so we beat *them*."

Jeffery looked thoughtful for a moment, then perked up in recognition. "Wait a sec, I know that line! War of the Worlds," he said.

"And would it surprise you to know that I was a child once and quite enjoyed that old movie?" Agent Hessman supplied. "Concentrate on the problem at hand."

"Then I suggest everyone look casual," Captain Beck said. "Look."

The rest followed the direction of his gaze to see a two-inch silvery ball moving along a fixed track down the length of the train car along the middle of its ceiling. They were seated at the back, but the device was already halfway to them.

"Camera," Jeffery told them quietly. "Same type I mentioned earlier."

Ben saw the camera coming this way, looked at Claire beside him with her large white hat and long dress, and did the first thing he could think of. He bent over to give her a kiss, using his entire body to block her from view and keeping the back of his head over her face. Agent Hessman took the cue and turned to face Captain Beck as if in conversation, a move which partially blocked both their faces. The ball came to the end of its track, paused for a moment, and then started sliding back toward the front.

Once it was far enough away Ben released his lip-lock of Claire, who gasped for air.

"I know we're going to be married," she said, "but I'd not think this an appropriate situation to get passionate."

"Not that I don't mind the excuse, mind you," Ben replied, "but from what we've learned from Jeffery here, your face is well known in certain circles. Circles which might—"

"Be hooked up to what that thing can see," Claire finished for him. "I got it. But if I'm known, then your face might also be."

"Hence my expedient solution."

"Congratulations on the quick thinking," Agent Hessman blandly remarked, "but I think our stop is coming up. Buckle up."

The train underwent a spine-crushing deceleration, and soon they were walking out of the train for their first view of Heathrow, though making sure to keep their faces down in the event that the device which had earlier tried to pick them out was still active. They came out into a terminal that let out directly below the Heathrow concourse, up a flight of steps, and into the main lobby.

The concourse was a vast circle sprouting nearly a hundred different exits around its circumference, each leading to a dozen different possibilities. Thousands of people were coming and going, some going up any of the dozens of escalators or elevators to higher levels of the concourse. Around the center of the huge area was a ring of reception desks and public computer terminals a hundred feet across, each with a line of people, while around the far-flung periphery of the concourse, in between the hundred exits, was a broken ring of shops, cafés, and other airport necessities. A glance up showed that the ceiling stretched away into glassy heights at least a dozen stories up, and from there out to unknown regions of the spaceport.

"I used 'wow' before, right?" Claire asked. "Anyone got anything better?"

"Working on it," Ben replied, he as struck with disbelief as she was. "It looks like they added to it a bit the last hundred years."

"I should say so," Captain Beck put in with a slow, amazed nod.

Jeffery led the way over to one of many sections of couches tossed around the place, one not yet occupied.

"Just wait here while I get the travel cards from one of the terminals. It shouldn't take long."

They watched as he ran off to stand in line for one of the computer terminals. Then they resumed their amazed visual perusal of their surroundings, though in Agent Hessman's case it may have been more for possible threat assessments.

"We stay strictly together," he finally said. "While there is no doubt several automated means are available for those separated from their party to find one another, that would involve means that others could use to find *us*."

"Agreed," Ben said once he had stifled his amazement. "I wonder what the airport itself is like."

"You mean this isn't it?" Claire asked.

"This is just the concourse, love—the place people go to find their way across to their flights. Everything else is somewhere outside."

Claire just slowly shook her head and held on more tightly to Ben.

A few minutes later Jeffery returned with a handful of cards, passing one out to each person there. "These are your travel cards," he explained.

"They look like credit cards," Captain Beck remarked.

"They're just small computerized cards that contain all your passage info. You can scan it across any public reader around here, and the screen will direct you to where you need to go if you're lost. No chip implant needed at this point. Passage includes the suborbital and back, with an option for coming down in the space elevator if you want to return that way instead. I got the best credits that my university friends could pool together. Now, you start off at gate thirty-four, which is . . . over this way."

As Jeffery led the way across the concourse with hurried steps, Agent Hessman asked a pertinent question, which he knew was on everyone's mind: "Space elevator?"

"Oh, still experimental, but if you need to come straight down from orbit in a couple of minutes, then that's the way. I didn't sign you up for going up in it because the only terminal for it is way out in the Equator."

"Got it. It's our emergency evac. Now for my next question: About your pals?"

Jeffery grinned as they walked along, and said, "For the record, depending on which of them you ask, this is all either for some super-secret conspiracy bust or the best prank against a certain rival school ever pulled."

Gate 34 was one of the multitude of passages leading off from the vast concourse; a wide tunnel that led out a hundred feet to a small terminal just large enough for the three gates arranged in a row, each of which held a waiting travel pod on a track leading down its own individual tube. Jeffery indicated the central one and the card reader before it.

"Each of you scan your cards as you climb on, then sit down and press the red button," he explained. "The travel tube will race you across the spaceport to your shuttle, where you can get directly on board. If ever in doubt—"

"We use our travel cards and the nearest public data reader," Agent Hessman finished for him. "Got it."

"This is also where I have to leave you." Jeffery sighed. "I need to stay behind, but you have everything you need now."

"We understand," Captain Beck replied.

He was the first one to step up and slide his card beneath the reader. Then, as the little gate swung open before him, Agent Hessman was next behind him.

"Oh, Jeffery," Claire told him, "I'll miss you. Thank you for helping us out. I know it was such a risk for you."

"Risk? It's been a blast! I got to help out *Claire Hill*, cross-temporal reporter. But if you don't mind, could you do *one* little thing for me?"

"Anything."

He turned his laptop over and produced a pen.

"Could you autograph my datapad before you leave, Miss Hill?"

"Why, of course."

Taking the offered pen, she did just that, signing her name boldly across the back of the datapad, then handing back the pen. Ben was just about to urge her along when Jeffery flipped the laptop back over.

"Wait a sec."

Slipping quickly in next to her, he held up his pad before them both. A quick flash of light from the top of the pad, then he stepped away. A second later a slender electronic card slid out of a port on the side of the laptop, which he handed to Claire.

"A memento to add to your collection. They say you were always collecting little keepsakes of whenever you went."

As he laid it flat on her palm, an image projected above it of him and her together, looking as solid as the real thing but in miniature. Claire smiled with delight at it, then reached out to give him a quick peck on the cheek before pocketing it and slipping into the pod after Ben.

"I'll never forget it or you, Jeffery. And tell that hacker friend of yours thank you from me."

"Oh, I'll be seeing her later on this evening." He grinned. "She's actually my girlfriend."

Her card flashed across beneath the reader, she sat down with the rest; then Captain Beck reached over to slap a hand onto a large red button on the inside of their pod. Immediately it sped off down the long tube, but this time everyone was well strapped in. It was the last Jeffery Nezsmith would see of any of them, but not the last he would *hear* of them: he would continue to read the many articles that were penned by her hand.

"Wow, Claire Hill! Jan's never going to believe this. And she just might kill me for not telling her up front."

The pod bore its four passengers along the tube, across the vast reach of the airport, and was quickly lost from sight.

16

SEDATING THE PRISONER

Samantha Weiss awoke to find herself stretched out on a cold, hard plastic slab.

She did not move at first, or even open her eyelids, but rather remained still and simply listened. She could hear voices talking around her, men speaking in what sounded like Russian. She listened for a bit to place the locations of the voices and, from their echo, get an approximate idea of the size of the room she was in. It didn't feel like a big room, perhaps between twenty and thirty feet across, and it sounded like three men—no, four; another man with a different quality to his voice had just started speaking to the others.

From what she could tell, they were gathered at a distance past her feet, conversing in low tones. It didn't feel like they had strapped her down, so depending on where the exit was, she might be able to make a run for it. She just had to be careful of those electrified bullets of theirs. She felt okay, no dizziness, drug aftereffects, or weakness of limb. Just a slight pinching feeling at the back of her neck.

She carefully tensed each of her arm and leg muscles to make sure all was in readiness, felt her pulse quicken, then snapped open her eyes while rolling over to one side, off the slab, and onto her feet.

The room was white, lit overhead by bright recessed lighting. Behind her the bulk of the wall was one large mirror, which she guessed to be two-way, up until a door to her left, at the far end. Mounted on the ceiling was something like a lighting fixture except in place of light bulbs from it projected a number of medical-looking mechanical arms, currently folded back into place around the core. To either side of the room stood more medical-looking equipment on wheeled carts; biometric monitors and such, one of which looked like a heart-rate monitor, which suddenly spiked at her motion. Then ahead of her were the four men, gathered into a small huddle between her and what looked like a sliding door with a keypad lock.

The instant she saw the heart-rate monitor jump she knew what that pinched feeling at her neck must be and quickly reached back and pulled off whatever was there. Sure enough, it was some sort of computer chip with needle legs that had been stuck into her flesh. The moment it was removed, the heart-rate monitor went dead.

The men turned at her movement, one of them reaching to his waist for something holstered there as she threw the chip at them and rushed to the nearest equipment cart. On it were devices with small screens, oscilloscopes, computerized drip-feeds, and other functions she cared not about, just that they were heavy. One cart, then two she sent rolling at them, then ran around the back side of the table she had been lying on and sent the first cart there crashing toward them.

One of the men was the same man she had seen as a floating head in her new lab; two others she recognized from the brief encounter at the Los Alamos conference. The fourth man, though, was new. One of them ran around to her right, another to the left, while a third remained by the exit along with the new man. All were dark-haired, heavyset Russians, save the new one, who was a little skinnier than the others.

The carts smashed into them and were quickly swatted away, but it bought her a precious second or two to think. There was a door behind her, to one side of the mirror wall, but it was probably locked. Still, it was a better chance than trying to bulldoze her way through these four men.

She leaped over to the door by the mirror wall, but when she looked for a doorknob she found nothing but a flat surface. That and a pad in the wall just to one side.

"Palm scanner," she swore.

Spinning quickly around, she brought her foot up in a sweeping kick before bothering to see if there was anyone there to hit. The man who had charged up on this side of the room had indeed made it past the hurtling cart and gotten close enough for her foot to smack against the side of his chin. He let out a growl of pain, then lunged.

Samantha leaped feetfirst, but not at her attacker. Instead, she landed on her back, sliding across the floor past him, beneath reach of his grasping arms. Once past she rolled quickly up to her feet, grabbed one of the heavier-looking equipment carts, and, using it like a battering ram, charged straight at the pair by the exit, pushing the wheeled cart before her. She thought to slam it into them and then, while they were picking themselves up, worry about the keypad.

What happened was the larger of the two braced himself and caught the other side of the cart with both hands and snarled at her as his far-larger muscles easily absorbed the impact. A moment later he shoved the cart aside, leaving nothing between them.

She had to think fast. She was still dressed as she had been when they took her, which meant that she still had whatever was in her pockets at the time. As she stepped back, she reached in and pulled out the first thing her fingers grabbed on to. It was a pen.

"Stay back," she warned. "I got a ball-point."

She held it up like a knife in her right hand, ready to stab down at the first one to come at her. Instead, at a sharp command from the thinner man they all paused. She was surrounded, her back to the wall, and with nothing effective on hand to defend herself with.

"Anyone comes near me and I'll make sure you feel a lot of pain."

In response, the three men from before reached to their belts and pulled out their pistols and aimed them right at her. Two of them were within reach, but the third one across the room could get her before she could get near him. The only one without a weapon was the fourth, skinnier man, who now spoke in lightly accented English.

"Miss Weiss, you must realize that there is no way out for you. Now, if you'll please stop struggling; this equipment you've been tossing around can be quite expensive."

"What do you want with me?"

She still had her pen out like a knife, body slightly crouched and awaiting any opportunity that might present itself.

"You're prepping me for an operation of some sort. Why?"

"Simple enough," the man calmly replied. "To save our present we need *you* to change our past, Miss Weiss."

"Well, if it's cooperation you want, you're not getting it. And I doubt I'll be hanging around here long enough for you to force me."

"Ah yes, you mean the team sent forward to rescue you." The man smiled. "They should be right on schedule despite the best efforts of the temporal police. We should be done by the time they arrive to save you, Miss Weiss. Now, if you'll kindly put down that pen, we can get started."

Samantha slowly shook her head, backing up a step until her heel hit the wall. "You're going to have to—"

Three shots rang out, three times an electrical snap whizzed through the air, and three times an electrified bullet hit her body, sticking like a dart to deliver its charge. Her body convulsed, the pen flying out of her hand, and then her joints froze, spilling her to the ground to convulse some more before she finally went limp.

"Now, as I was saying, get her properly sedated and prepped," the thinner man calmly ordered. "We haven't much time."

17

SPACE VEGAS

The pod sped them through the tube, not as fast as the bullet train but fast enough that sitting strapped in was the only option. It was a second or two before the walls cleared into transparency, allowing them a view of the spaceport across which they sped.

Theirs was one of several such tubes, all radiating from the central hub, like spokes on a wheel, to the far-flung points of the port. The port looked like a large concrete desert stretching out to some distant green hills. The endpoint of each tube was always the same: what looked like a sleek delta-winged aircraft hooked up to its terminal tube by a covered platform and retractable corrugated umbilical. Theirs was no exception, for ahead of them they could see the craft that they now approached.

"I thought we were headed up into space," Claire remarked. "Didn't you say that involves a tall, pointy rocket?"

"Space travel has apparently evolved," Ben replied. "Rocketry isn't my field, and unfortunately, Sam's not with us."

"Fortunately, high-security military projects are *my* field," Captain Beck put in, "and that thing looks like an advanced development of some concepts we got rolling around. The space shuttle was only meant as a stepping-stone. The endgame is to have a system that has no need of a rocket to get up into space, but is a completely reusable system from start to finish. This looks like we finally achieved that goal. Probably takes off much like that bullet train we felt, then angles straight up."

"Whatever it involves, just act like all this is perfectly normal to us so we don't stand out," Agent Hessman cautioned.

"Nonsense," Claire decided. "That's a sure-fire way *to* stand out."

"Miss Hill, our goal is not to be noticed."

"First off, in a few months it's going to be 'Miss Stein,' so get used to it," she corrected, "and second, the name is *Claire*."

"Claire," Agent Hessman reluctantly addressed her.

"It's like what I'm wearing versus you guys. Or going to the board-walk. You remember when we were at Steeplechase Park? Did you ever see anyone there looking bored, like they'd seen it all? No, they were all excited. We're going on vacation to *Space Vegas* on our first trip into orbit. Who can act bored for something like that in *any* century?"

That said, she relaxed back into her seat, satisfied that her argument had been won. From the looks on the men's faces, it had been. As their pod began to slow with its approach to their terminal, Captain Beck leaned over for a quiet word with Claire.

"You'll have to excuse Lou. He doesn't do 'excited vacationer' very well."

Their pod came to a halt at a terminal similar to where they had boarded. As they exited their pod, a stewardess was there to help them out and welcome them with a smile.

"Welcome to Virgin Spaceways' flight to Space Vegas. You must be the party from the university."

"Yes," Agent Hessman began, all seriousness. "We're here to check out—"

"Space Vegas!" Claire said with a hop to her step. "Oh, I'm so excited!"

"First-time visitors, I see," the stewardess said as she led the way. "They're always so enthusiastic."

Claire flashed Lou a quick grin. Then Ben got willingly into the act and wrapped an arm around her waist. "We're actually here to celebrate," he said. "I just asked her the question," whereupon Claire held up her left hand and flashed her new ring with a bright smile.

The stewardess replied with a nod and motioned them onward. "Congratulations, Miss. Now, if you'll just step across the gantry, you can be in Space Vegas in no time and begin your new lives together."

The gantry was a simple metal walkway leading from the terminal chamber, guardrails on the sides, but it was surrounded by a corrugated rubberlike tube that reached out the entire length, sealed at the far end in a circular housing around an open metal aircraft door and another smiling stewardess. Agent Hessman was ready to lead the way, but Claire nearly dragged Ben on ahead, giggling as she went. She was the first to produce her travel card for the spaceline stewardess waiting at the other end, the terminal number floating in bright numbers in the air above her.

The lady produced a hand scanner and flashed it across the card, then reached for Ben next in line as she greeted them. "Welcome aboard. My name is Tiffany and I'll be your stewardess for the duration of this trip. If there is anything you need, just say so."

She scanned Agent Hessman's card next, then lastly Captain Beck's, and he did have a question.

"Uh, I have a question, Miss. If you're prone to seasickness, will this . . ."

"If you feel nauseated while we're in flight, just hit your call button and I'll be right there with a little something to fix you up."

The interior reminded Agent Hessman of a jumbo jet, the main differences being that the seats were bulkier and a lot more padded and arranged on a gimbal system for reclining.

"Nice crash couches," Ben remarked.

There were windows along the sides of the craft, just as in a normal airplane, and all the usual accoutrements one would expect of a plane. The floor was even carpeted.

"It looks like you're going to be the only passengers today," Tiffany said as she thumbed a red button to the side of the door, "so feel free to sit anywhere you like."

"Window seat," Claire immediately called out. "I want to see the takeoff."

The door slid automatically into place, after which Tiffany rotated a large lever beside the red button down into place to lock it. Claire got her window seat, with Ben sitting beside her, while Captain Beck and Agent Hessman took the seats immediately behind them, though the captain did not take the window seat.

Shortly after the stewardess secured herself in a seat at the rear, a male voice called out through the speakers: *"This is your captain speaking. We're going to be taxiing out to our runway for takeoff; then it's off for Space Vegas. We should be achieving orbit in approximately three minutes and then arrive at the station thirty minutes after that. Enjoy the trip."*

They felt the motion of the craft as it taxied into position. They could see the runway ahead of them through the window and felt the craft turning to align itself, then a brief pause.

They were slammed back into their seats, the view outside becoming a blur. The cabin was insulated, but even so, they could still hear the faint echo of a sharp whine. Then came a slight buoyant feeling as the craft began to lift off the ground. For several seconds they sped on and up. When they dared glance out the window the ground had grown quite distant and the entirety of the port could be seen as a large relief-map of itself.

"Hold on tight, folks. That was just the first step. We're going into orbit now, but don't worry; those acceleration couches will automatically adjust. You'll only feel a little more pull."

"What does he mean by 'a little more'?" Captain Beck asked.

The craft suddenly curved into a sharp arch, aiming itself straight up with a rumble of power they could feel through the floor. Their seats automatically tilted to partially compensate for the angle, and they found the padding more than sufficient to absorb the impact of their acceleration. Even so, movement of anything but one's eyeballs was not an option.

Through the corner of her eye, Claire could see the ground speed away until the entire outline of England came into view, storms and all.

She tried to giggle in awe and delight, but movement was still restricted. Agent Hessman, though, was noticing other things. Things like the full reach of the London dike system and what a mammoth project it was, and the oversized reach of a couple of hurricanes covering the Atlantic nearly from shore to shore.

By the time three minutes had passed the acceleration suddenly lifted and they found themselves afloat above the earth.

"You can now undo your restraints, folks, and walk around if you wish, but I advise you to keep to your seats. The trip will only take us half an hour, so just enjoy the flight. Tiffany will now come around to see if any of you want anything to drink."

Claire was all delight, snapping off the restraint button so she could get a better view of what lay outside. She was still staring openmouthed when she noticed something: her large hat was floating up off her head. "My hat!"

"It's the gravity," Ben told her. "We don't have any."

"Well, it is a very strange feeling, let me tell you. You don't find this unusual?"

"Oh, very. We're both in the same boat on this one. Er, spaceship rather."

"About time. Oh, there's Europe. But look at all those clouds."

While Claire was ogling the view, with Ben looking over her shoulder for his own stunning glimpse, Agent Hessman was giving it a more methodical study. Captain Beck opted for avoiding the view when the stewardess, Tiffany, came walking by.

They could feel the weightlessness, and Claire finally had to take off her hat and hold it against her chest, but Tiffany seemed to have little trouble with it. She was walking slowly, each step deliberate as she approached. "Would any of you like something to drink?" she asked.

Agent Hessman glanced over to see that her shoes had something resembling Velcro on the bottom soles to grip her into place, while Captain Beck had a more pleading expression.

"Scotch?"

"You're just nervous," she stated. "Here, this should help."

She handed him a small pill, which he immediately swallowed and then did his best to relax back into the chair.

For Claire and Ben, the next thirty minutes were an unending parade of orbital sights, their windows automatically opaquing against the power of the sun when required. For Agent Hessman it was more of a studied examination of the world as a whole, though he was not above admitting to himself to a certain amount of awe at the sights.

The first thing Agent Hessman noticed, however, was the vibrations coming from one of his pockets. He reached in and discreetly pulled out his time beacon and checked the readout on its front along with the red flashing light. Putting it back, he leaned in to address the others.

"Our beacons are now out of range. If we ever need to use them, we'll have to get planetside first."

"No quick exits," Captain Beck stated. "If we get hurt up here, then . . . Well, we don't have Dr. Weiss here to tell us the possibilities."

"We'll be careful," Ben agreed.

"That's still not going to get in the way of my enjoying all this," Claire said. "Would you just *look* at all that out there . . ."

The warning noted, Claire went back to gazing out the window, while Captain Beck felt the little pill easing his nervous stomach. Half an hour later an announcement came from their captain that directed their attention to an even brighter spectacle.

"We are on final approach to Space Vegas, so if you'll just strap in while we match rotation, you can catch a great view of it. I personally never tire of this sight."

Ben had imagined a boxy little station, cramped and confined, such as what astronauts in the movies swam through, and Claire had no preconception at all. What they saw, though, exceeded any expectation or lack thereof. It was a vast plate, as if someone had taken an entire city and covered it. The center portion was a solid disc a few miles across and what looked to be several stories tall, with windows dotting its sides. From the center a large shaft grew both up from the top and down through the bottom. A shaft that Captain Beck was certain would be thick enough on which to park the main core of the little international space station from back in 2020 with room to rattle. The upper shaft stretched up a thousand feet before ending at another disc, this one maybe half a mile across and five stories tall. The lower shaft likewise ended at a third disc that was about half the width and height of the main disc.

Scattered around the outer perimeter of the main disc were what looked like docking mechanisms with massive clamps to secure the crafts and extendable airlocks and gantries ready to reach out and lock on, some of which already had vessels similar to their own parked in place.

Then there were the lights. At the very top of the upper disc a large red ball was brightly shining. A beacon of some sort, no doubt, but that was the least of it. In typical Old Vegas style, this station was far from being the drab gray metal military port some would have been. Lights lit up in rows running completely around the main disc, flowing in colored patterns that made it seem like a large sparkling gem. In the open region between the main and upper discs, holographic projections hovered in place, rotating with the station. Letters the size of buildings spelled out the name SPACE VEGAS, accompanied by fireworks-like displays and all the glitz one could ask for.

Between the main and lower disc hovered a series of smaller holographic signs, each advertising one hotel or attraction or another to approaching visitors. Takeoffs on Old Vegas names rotated slowly around the hub—The Astral, The Stratosphere, The Galaxy—some along with the names of supposedly famous acts performing there, though all the names were lost on those now watching. The lower disc itself was lit up with blue and silver running lights flashing around in swift circles, then pausing before reversing direction or briefly changing to a fixed pattern.

Taken as a whole, Space Vegas was enough to render everyone silent as it loomed closer. Even Claire was stuck for words.

As their craft got closer, its course altered to run parallel to the main disc, carefully sliding in closer while matching the rotation of the station. Closer in they could see that this disc was even taller than it had seemed from afar, and anything but slender.

"That must be fifty stories high," Ben finally managed to utter.

Beside him Claire could only absently nod while her jaw hung open

Space Vegas Exterior

Space Vegas Interior

"Well," Captain Beck said with a swallow, "leave it to Vegas to do things right. Lou?"

"Okay, so color me impressed," Agent Hessman admitted. "But that's a lot of space to search."

As their course came to match the circular rotation of the great station, Claire's hat drifted gently down into her lap and that odd feeling in their stomachs started to ease up. Closer they got until it was a vast, glittering wall before them. Aiming for one of the airlocks, they carefully approached, slipping gently in, until they were running parallel with it. The large mechanical clamp reached out for the front of the vessel, coming down surprisingly gently. Then a dull thud was felt, the sound ringing through the hull, and they watched as the gantry started reaching out. It was basically a square metal tube with an airlock door at its end surrounded by a thick rubber seal and a series of small clamps. It reached toward their cabin door; then moments later an even softer impact was heard, then a sharp hiss from just beyond the heavy door. All sense of motion ceased, weight returned to their feet, and the captain's voice once again came out over the cabin speakers.

"We have docked. You may get up and leave the cabin just as soon as Tiffany opens the airlock door. You will find that the rotation of the station approximates Earth's gravity when around the outer perimeter. Don't forget any of your belongings, and have a great time at Space Vegas.

Claire nearly bolted to her feet, pushing Ben ahead of her, in her eagerness to see what lay beyond. Captain Beck, though, looked more relieved than eager. "At least my stomach feels normal again," he stated.

A turn of the lock, a press of the red button, and the door automatically slid aside, revealing not a cold, metallic gantry but a plush, velvet-lined, brightly lit walkway with red carpeting beckoning them to enter.

"Ooh, the red-carpet treatment." Claire beamed. "I feel like royalty."

"You *look* like royalty," Ben couldn't help but reply.

Adjusting her floppy white sunhat and smoothing her dress, Claire was the first to step out onto the walkway, her face lit up with a smile nearly as bright as the lights ahead of them. Agent Hessman came alongside Ben as they passed Tiffany on their way out, with Captain Beck at their rear.

Once they were midway down the hall, Agent Hessman discreetly checked the detector in his pocket and was rewarded by a short readout. "We're within range of Samantha's locator chip," he whispered to the others. "She's definitely somewhere on this station."

"Tracking her should be pretty straightforward then," Captain Beck remarked. "How exact a fix can you get on her?"

"Not very. There's any number of electronic signals interfering around here and a lot to look through from the looks of it. Best we have is a proximity alarm."

As they approached the end of the walkway, ahead of them it opened up into a whole world of lights, sparkle, and glitter.

"It still shouldn't be too bad, though," Captain Beck said.

Ben and Claire came to a sudden stop where the velvet hallway joined the expanse beyond.

"Uh, you ever been to Las Vegas, Robert?" Ben asked hesitantly. "Because I think we have a problem."

Captain Beck and Agent Hessman stepped up to join Ben and Claire for their first view of Space Vegas. The cavernous expanse of the foyer reached two hundred feet across, several stories up, and as many down, and was festooned with walkways with glass guard walls, platforms sporting rest stops with seating and computer-terminal kiosks, glass elevators scattered about, and a multitude of people milling about. Across the open gap they could see the edges of one level upon another, some with various bars and cafés running the length of their walkways, others with brightly lit corridors heading deeper into the innards of the station. The open foyer didn't stop until five or six levels down, where it ended at some sort of promenade, and five or six levels above their heads, at a ceiling through which stairwells and more glass-covered elevators led.

Silvery balls hung suspended in the air between levels, around some of which floated images of either some local performer or directions to whatever hangout paid for the advertising. Music played, whatever the hit of the day happened to be, interrupted by the occasional announcement of flight numbers leaving or arriving, calling for some lost person to report to a numbered concierge desk, or simply welcoming visitors to Space Vegas.

Across at some of the bars hovered more holographic displays, as well as others beckoning down one hall or another. In short, the whole place sparkled; it was the Las Vegas Strip rendered in 3D, and this was just one foyer in a vast three-dimensional city.

The wild clothing they had seen in London now seemed tame by comparison, though, in truth, most of the more revealing outfits looked to be worn by employees of the adjacent cafés, bars, and gambling establishments. Statuesque young women in short-skirted, transparent dresses lit up by their own shifting displays that danced around the hidden portions of their beauty; hairdos that flowed with a life of their own, their colors gradually shifting from blond to brunette and back again; patrons in long dresses woven of shifting patterns of light, and one whose dress was barely a few strategically placed strips of lights and no cloth at all—this was just a sampling of the women's fashion on display. Men passed by with their own unique looks, from glowing ten-gallon hats and foot-long handlebar mustaches to faux-leather jackets decorated with rhinestones that gleamed from their own inner lights.

It was a degree of glamor that stunned all there and had Claire looking shyly away from some of the passersby.

"It's like Vegas times ten," Ben stated when he could speak again.

"And this is just one of the entries," Captain Beck said slowly in agreement.

"Would you look at what some of those people are wearing?" Claire remarked. "Someone was worried about how *I* might look? I'm starting to feel like the guy in the business suit."

"I guess that explains the electrical interference," Agent Hessman stated, "but we may have another problem."

"You mean this isn't enough?" Ben asked.

"Ten o'clock left and two levels down," Agent Hessman directed.

All eyes followed his directions, across and down, to the sporty entrance to one of the glamorous hotels; something with an apparent

Egyptian theme. Alongside greeters dressed like Cleopatra and Marc Antony, they saw a couple of men in uniform—blue-and-green uniforms with a symbol on their chests that looked like three concentric rings around a capital T.

"The time cops from London," Captain Beck said. "They're still trying to track us down."

"Yup," Agent Hessman stated, "and we have to evade them while looking for Samantha. This isn't going to be easy."

"It looks like Jeffery was right," Claire put in. "There's always a chase wherever we go. So, everyone ready?"

From the bright smile on her face, one might have thought she was looking forward to the encounter.

18

STATION RUN

Agent Hessman led the way onto the landing before them, picking a walkway off to their left.

"Just keep it casual," he cautioned. "They might not have spotted us yet. No reason to call attention to ourselves."

They started walking, though Claire's way of not calling attention to herself was to eagerly point at one sight or another and pull Ben along with her—basically, acting just like any other tourist. The walkway led them around the outer edge; to their right, a long window with a view of space that she could not help but pause to gape before.

"We're standing on infinity," she gasped. "Oh, Ben."

"I'll admit, I could stand here for hours just looking at it," Ben agreed.

Agent Hessman cut in: "I rather think we have a much shorter time than that. Our pursuers appear to have spotted us."

A glance across the foyer showed the two uniformed men riding up one of the glass elevators at the far side.

"We've got to run!" Claire gasped.

She already had her hand on her hat to hold it down and run, but Agent Hessman held her back.

"Quick walk, no running," he advised. "We don't want to stir up the locals, and I don't think they do either. It's their turf, and they know this is a closed environment with only so many places we can run to."

"Then what do we do?" Ben asked.

"We find a new place to run to. Follow me."

They quickened their pace, weaving through the crowd. A glance back showed that the two uniforms were just getting off their elevator on the same level as themselves and starting into the same quick walk. Agent Hessman led them left onto a crossing over a four-story drop to another landing. Pausing midway across one of the glass elevator tubes, he pressed a button before a clear door. Moments later the elevator came up and the doors slid aside. The uniforms were a couple hundred feet away when the doors closed behind them.

The inside had a panel like any elevator of their own day, with numbered buttons and a couple of service buttons on the bottom row. Lou immediately hit the highest-numbered button he could see. The two uniforms were still threading their way through the crowd when the elevator shot up out of sight.

They had a brief aerial view of the whole section when they shot up through the ceiling and up to the next level. In this brief interval between floors decorated with images of clouds projected all around them, they caught a fleeting glimpse of a level that looked like a glamorous food court done by way of Rodeo Drive, before they were gone again into the clouds and another level came into view. Here Agent Hessman slammed a hand onto a button marked with a large X. The elevator immediately came to a stop and eased down level with the floor.

"Everyone out," he ordered.

The last one out, Agent Hessman hit a random selection of buttons, then slipped out before the doors closed shut and the elevator zoomed away.

"Old trick," he stated. "Now just start walking."

This section had a large open floor across which people came and went as they looked over the selections that circled them. It looked like a ring of high-class restaurants. On the left was one labeled "NY, NY" with projected images of the Statue of Liberty and other local landmarks of note, with a miniature reproduction of the Brooklyn Bridge sized perfectly for two people to walk across over a pretend river. A hundred feet past that one was a place with an underwater theme named Atlantis, followed by Hard Rock Café fifty feet later on the far side. Completing the other half of the circle was The Fifth Season, Gordon's Grill, and The Player. Off to their right, a wide hall curved farther around the perimeter, with a holographic sign flashing "Rail."

"Expensive eats," Claire remarked.

"We're not staying to eat," Agent Hessman replied. "The rail."

They hurried over to the hall on the right, stepping quickly along the carpeted floor until the curvature brought them out of sight of the restaurants and into view of what looked like a transit-pod station like back at Heathrow. There was a short line of people waiting as one long pod would speed into view from out of a tunnel in the left-hand wall, then pause to deposit its passengers and admit new ones before whizzing off through the wall to the right.

"I have no doubt that they can track our temporal signatures better than we can track Samantha," Agent Hessman said as they fell into line, "so this will be challenging."

"More so since we have neither their Net links nor any of their money," Ben observed. "Just these transport cards."

"If I'm right, that should be enough. If this is like *our* Las Vegas, they're going to be comping a lot of stuff to keep people moving toward the casinos and shows."

Their turn in line came up as the next pod slid into place to deposit its travelers. The gate opened before them, no card or money needed.

"Such as free transportation?" Ben ventured.

Once inside the pod, a map was projected in the air before them, with one dot to indicate their current location. Captain Beck pressed a finger uncertainly into the air, stabbing at a point away from the outer perimeter. Immediately the pod started moving. A swift flight through the wall and across what the holograms would have them believe to be soaring mountain heights was followed by a dive down into a deep rocky core.

"Even the cabs around this place are entertaining," Ben remarked with a grin.

"If you like motion sickness," Captain Beck replied.

"I think it's *wonderful!*" Claire exclaimed. "I feel like an eagle."

Agent Hessman, meanwhile, was back to looking at his tracker. "Still not close enough," he stated, "though this tube is a good way to cover a lot of ground quickly. If I call out, someone make note of where the map says we are, and get this thing to stop."

"Sure," Ben uncertainly replied, "just as soon as I figure out how to work this thing."

They made one last pass through what the holograms made them believe to be a watery canal before emerging into another rail station similar to the first. This time they stepped out into the middle of what looked like a circus and an arcade mall, with performers leaping through the air in their wire acrobatics, mechanical elephants giving rides to young kids, game booths strewn about a busy promenade, and of course the obligatory scantily clad young women there to direct people to the various activities.

"It's just like Steeplechase!" Claire gasped.

"Only a few stories taller," Captain Beck noted.

"Ooh," Claire began, "can we—"

"No rides," Ben said.

"Actually, a ride may be just what we need," Agent Hessman stated.

They glanced through the crowd to where he'd indicated with a nod of his head. Across the open arcade of game booths, rides, and entertainment, with its crowd of thousands, they spied two men in certain specific uniforms.

"How'd they even find us, much less make it up here before us?" Ben wondered.

"Multiple teams," Agent Hessman answered. "But what I find more interesting is that roller-coaster ride over there."

He led a hurried pace through the crowd to where a short line had formed for a multistory roller-coaster ride themed after rocket ships flying through an asteroid field. To the head of the line they hurried, with Agent Hessman making an odd remark to Claire: "Miss Hill, your hat needs adjusting."

"What? Oh, thank you."

As they approached the ride entrance, Claire made a small fuss of adjusting her large white sun hat while Agent Hessman glanced toward the pair of time cops. It didn't take much for them to notice Claire adjusting the wide brim into place.

"There, that looks better," she said.

"Good, they spotted us," Agent Hessman said.

"That's *good?*" Ben asked.

There was a young man controlling entry into the ride, and it was to him that Agent Hessman led the others while the time cops maneuvered as quickly as they could through the masses.

"Excuse me," Agent Hessman quickly addressed the young man, "but where is the chicken exit?"

"Just up ahead, but you aren't even in line yet, why would you—"

"Thank you."

Brushing past the young man, all four hurried for the indicated exit, but not before Agent Hessman grabbed the hat off Claire's head.

"Hey, my hat!"

Not bothering to reply, he slapped the large white hat on top of the nearest young woman about to board the ride.

"Present from Claire Hill, cross-temporal reporter," he told the woman.

Leaving a happy young woman behind them, Agent Hessman led them in a jog for the exit door and then a quick run down the hallway beyond.

"Distraction, Miss Hill—we needed one."

"I figured *that,*" she replied, "but you could have at least let me get my things out of it first."

"Your *things?*"

"Like I said before we left, a lady knows how to keep things under her hat."

"You mean you meant that literally?" Ben grinned.

"Why do you think I wore such a large hat? Small vial of chloroform, stun gun, hairpin—you'd be surprised how many things *those* are good for."

"Around you, Miss Hill, never."

After fifty feet the long metal corridor afforded a glass-walled view along their right of the shoot along which the coaster pods would streak as they shot into the main part of the ride. There they were able to see one pod go racing by sporting a happy young lady holding a large white hat tightly against her chest. The car after that held a pair of agents in uniform trying to keep an eye on the ones ahead of them.

That's when Claire stopped and rapped a few times hard against the glass wall, waving one hand in the air while smiling down at the two agents. In the brief time they had as their pod passed by below, they looked up to see Claire in her pink-and-white dress, sans hat, and some familiar faces alongside her.

"Sorry you missed us," she called out.

As the two annoyed-looking men were sped away into the bowels of the ride, Agent Hessman pulled them away into a fast run down the empty corridor.

"No need to worry about crowds right now. Come on."

It wasn't long to the other end, but as they ran, they began to notice something odd. Their steps were getting lighter and longer.

"I know I've been trying to lose weight," Captain Beck remarked, "but this is ridiculous. I thought this place had artificial gravity."

"Produced by the spin of the station," Ben explained, "which means the closer we get to the central core—"

"The lighter we get," Agent Hessman completed. "That just might work for us."

They exited into another open foyer, though smaller than the first. This one had the usual array of walkways crossing by above and below, but there were also some people who opted instead for swimming through the air direct to their destination, a few of them with little personal jets on a belt that blasted out puffs of air to guide them. These jet belts were available at a concession stand across the foyer.

"We going to try getting a set of those jet belts to play around with?" Ben asked.

"No money," came Agent Hessman's reply. "Just jump."

"What?" a shocked Claire asked.

"We're close to zero gravity around here. Just hold on to one another."

Grabbing Claire's hand, Agent Hessman leaped just as she in turn quickly grabbed Ben's hand, then he Captain Beck's, forming a snake of four people, slipping through the air over the open foyer. Fear quickly turned to glee as Claire let out a whoop of delight, though Captain Beck was significantly less thrilled. There was nothing but open air below them; to their far left, an immense picture-window view of Earth; to their right, the foyer opened up to a large multilevel shopping gallery well over a thousand feet across. The foyer was only a hundred or so feet across and rounded to contain the merrymakers except at the one end that widened into the shopping gallery beyond.

Below them another pair of time cops were running for the concession booth with the jet belts.

"This is exhilarating," Claire declared.

"I feel like a bird," Ben echoed.

"I feel sick," Captain Beck added.

"We don't have much control, so try not to tumble," Agent Hessman called back. "And whatever you do, don't let go."

Their flight was a slow drift across and up to whatever destination Agent Hessman had aimed them, while below them the pair of time cops were strapping on their belts and leaping into the air to give chase. Between the two groups couples tumbled gaily about, families and their young ones laughed as they pretended to be birds.

They were midway across when they heard one of the time cops calling up from below as they neared.

"Stop! You're out of time."

Even Agent Hessman would have smirked had he not been focused on their course.

"They really should have thought their way through that line," Ben said, grinning. "I know what they mean, but . . ."

"Get ready for impact," Agent Hessman called back.

The impact came against the far wall, but not just any random part of it. At their approach, Agent Hessman carefully reached out his free hand and grabbed on to a large ventilation grill, one locked into place by a simple latch, which he now proceeded to twist open. It covered a duct easily large enough for them each to swim through.

Which a moment later they did, though with the cry of the time cops close behind them.

"Stop! You need to go back!"

The duct was some ten feet across and fell into an endless well that had Claire's grip on Ben tightening considerably. They hovered there for a moment before Agent Hessman slammed his feet against the other side, bent his knees, then launched himself downward. As each in turn hit the wall, they repeated the maneuver, all while trying to keep their grips on one another. Down they dropped, everyone but Agent Hessman apparently afraid that gravity might at any second retake control. Above them the two agents came into view, but they had their jet belts to aid them.

"We're gonna get swallowed," Claire said with a hard gulp. "I don't mind admitting I'm really afraid right now."

"You aren't the only one," Ben agreed. "Uh, Lou, those guys are going to catch up any second. You have anything specific in mind?"

"Not particularly," he admitted, "just that whatever's down in that direction, the tracker in my pocket is vibrating like crazy. Samantha's down there, so we're not stopping."

"Okay, I can see that," Ben said, "but, uh, *they* don't seem to be stopping either."

Down the nearly gravity-free shaft they fell, above them a pair of time cops closing in fast with pistols in hand, below them little more than a dimly lit pit.

19

RESCUE

"Everyone," Agent Hessman called out, "roll aside! Robert, your stun gun *now*."

Agent Hessman rolled to the left while reaching for something in his pocket, and Captain Beck rolled right, pulling out his Taser. Ben grabbed Claire and rolled with her away perpendicular to the other two just as one of their slowly gaining pursuers fired off an electrified bullet. The shot narrowly missed Agent Hessman as he threw out that which he had drawn out from his pocket. It was a small bottle of liquid.

Still descending in slow motion, Captain Beck spun around to face up, so that he was now falling backward, and fired his Taser. He was not, however, aiming for either of the two time cops. The twin darts shot out for the bottle, trailing long wires back to the pistol. It was a solid shot that hit the bottle dead on, but what might stun a person cannot shatter a bottle.

The other gunshot did.

The contents of the shattered bottle continued up along the bottle's original trajectory, but now spreading out into a wide spray that caught the pair of time cops full in the face. Nearly immediately their reactions began slowing. One of them tried to stay awake with a shake of his head as he fired off a shot from his pistol, a shot that went wild when his other hand sleepily brushed his jet-belt control, sending him spinning slowly around and his charged bullet homing in on another ventilation grid they were passing by.

Agent Hessman gave a satisfied look back before returning his attention to their course. "That chloroform should keep them busy for a while, but where did that gunshot come from?"

A guilty-looking Claire was falling backward a little faster now, with Ben holding her from behind; in her hand, a small derringer.

"My other things were in my hat, but I had this wrapped up in my scarf," she confessed. "I know it may be a bit outdated, and it was supposed to be nonlethal, but I thought maybe . . ."

"No time to argue with results," Agent Hessman replied. "Now let's see about our course."

While Ben tried to correct his and Claire's course, which had been altered by the diminutive kickback of the small pistol in near-zero gravity, Agent Hessman had his tracker in hand for a quick glance. Captain Beck pressed a small knob on his Taser to reel in the wires, then pocketed the weapon. Above them the pair of time cops were trying unsuccessfully to stay awake while absently fumbling at the controls of their jet belts.

"Just down a bit more," Agent Hessman said after a moment. "Follow me."

Kicking off against the side wall of the wide shaft, he shot down, leaving the two drugged time police well behind him. Ben and Claire did their best to roll down after him, while Captain Beck didn't seem much more skilled at the art of zero-gravity tumbling than they were. Agent Hessman aimed himself like a bullet, speeding down straight for another vent. As he neared it, he reached out his right hand. Counting down silently to himself, when he was nearly upon it, he rolled to his right and slammed out his hand.

He caught on to the inside of the shaft, his lower body arcing on past the rest of him until he was hanging by his arms from the edge of the adjoining vent. Only for a moment, though, as his legs kicked against the wall of the main shaft, his momentum then spent. As he proceeded to pull himself into the connecting shaft, Ben came up right behind him, one hand reaching out, the other wrapped around Claire's waist. Agent Hessman had pulled himself halfway in when he felt a sudden weight tugging on his right leg. He braced against it for a moment until he heard the sound of two joined bodies hitting lightly against the side wall of the main shaft, then finished pulling himself and now his two passengers all the way in.

Captain Beck came barreling straight into the shaft just as Ben was helping Claire in ahead of him. He came feetfirst into Ben's rear, and soon the lot of them were spilling through the vent until narrowing confines allowed them to stop their tumbling.

"Sorry about that," Captain Beck apologized, "but it's not like I had astronaut training."

"That was still a pretty good pool shot—right into the pocket," Ben replied. "Lou, how are we looking?"

Agent Hessman crawled on a bit before briefly consulting his tracker, giving room for the rest to space out. "On the right course," he announced. "Try and crawl as quietly as you can. No sense in alerting whoever may be up ahead."

They crawled as quietly as four grown adults could in a confined ventilation shaft, Ben coming up behind Agent Hessman for a quiet word.

"We really lucked out back there," he said. "I'm surprised those time police didn't manage to catch up with us with those jet belts before you got that bottle of chloroform off."

"Not too surprising, though a calculated risk," Agent Hessman admitted. "You saw the displays on the booth selling them, the kids and families playing around with them. They're toys, not designed for any sort of serious velocity even in such low gravity. True, it allowed them far better control of their direction, but we could gain better acceleration by pushing off against the walls."

"I never would have thought of that. Guess that's why you're the leader."

"And as your leader, from what my tracker is telling me as to the distance ahead, we should be feeling some gravity returning by the time we get there. So please warn Miss Hill back there that the time for giggling like a kid is coming to an end."

A glance back did indeed show Claire quite enjoying herself as she pretended to be a fish swimming through the sea of zero gravity. Ben dropped back and placed a finger to his lips to quiet her, but while she did come to a halt and resume a more normal crawl, she pulled his finger away from his mouth and replaced it with her own lips in a quick kiss.

"What was that for? Not that I mind, of course."

"For being you," she replied, "for being here for me. These past few months I've been feeling out of place, away from everything and everyone I'd ever known. But you've been making me feel like it's perfectly normal for a girl to be wandering through time with her fiancé. I wouldn't have survived without you, and a ventilation shaft in some futuristic space station seemed as good a place as any to reward you. You are my knight."

"Well then, my lady, might I return the favor?"

"You may," she giggled.

While Ben and Claire made their exchanges, in the lead Agent Hessman had his eye on his tracker. Two sets of branching shafts he ignored, and as they crawled, they all could indeed feel a portion of their weight gradually returning. After what seemed like an interminable length of time for crawling, he waved a hand back, motioning the others to stop, then pointed ahead of himself. Twenty feet ahead their small shaft came to an end at a grid.

He placed a finger to his lips, the others quieting in response, then led the crawl with far more silent care. When he was a few feet away from the grid he carefully looked through, then backed away and lay down on his back with feet drawn in and aimed at the ventilation grid, hands pushing against the sides of the shaft ready to launch himself forward.

A sharp kick and the grid flew off. He then launched himself into the room beyond, whipping out his Taser after landing.

It looked to be a small control room, with computers, monitors, displays, and one large shaded window off to his right. A couple of the displays were showing what appeared to be bio-sign readings, from a

Clair & Ben Kissing while floating

heart-rate monitor to a brain-wave pattern. There was one tech sitting at the controls, his attention fixed on the view through the window, when Agent Hessman burst in. The man had time enough to turn and gasp at the entry before two electrified darts trailing wires stuck into his body and had him briefly spasming before slumping into unconsciousness. Agent Hessman was just reeling the wires of his Taser back in when Ben slipped out of the shaft behind him, followed by Claire and Captain Beck.

"So where are we?" Ben asked.

Agent Hessman gestured in the direction of the window, then leaped toward the one door leading into the room beyond. Ben stepped forward to see, then beside him heard Claire gasp at the same sight. It was an operation room, at the center of which was Samantha Weiss strapped down to a table.

"What are they doing to her?" Claire wondered.

The end of the room had two doors out: the one into the operation room and another. As Agent Hessman burst through the one into the operation room, Captain Beck charged forward to hold the door open behind him and give the other door a hard look. Ben took the hint and hurried over to examine the other door.

There were two men in medical whites in the room, one of whom received Agent Hessman's fist in his face. They were hovering around some equipment by the operating table, preparing their unconscious patient for . . . something. The other man said something in Russian, while making a grab for something on a handy operating tray, and received Agent Hessman's other fist as he turned back around. This was followed by a swift kick.

Claire was observing through the two-way mirror that was the control room's window, watching Agent Hessman thrash the pair of Russian medical staffers, and could not help but smile. "He really loves her. I just hope he doesn't wait too long before asking her on a date. A girl will wait only so long."

Ben, meanwhile, was finding that the other door out operated with a simple button to open it, no hand scanner required when leaving from the inside. He soon had the door open a crack to see what was outside, then held it closed.

With both men on the ground, Agent Hessman turned his attention to Samantha. She lay on the large plastic slab, restraints holding down hands and feet, eyes closed. Working quickly, he undid the straps, then propped up her head with one hand while gently slapping her face with the other.

"Samantha, come on, wake up. It's Lou Hessman."

Her eyes flickered briefly, adjusting into a look of recognition, then a brief smile before faintly whispering, "Back of neck."

He felt around, found the chip-like device pinned into her neck, and pulled it out. Immediately her limbs seemed to relax while the bio-monitors all flatlined.

"Lou," Captain Beck called in, "no telling how much time we have."

Agent Hessman helped Samantha to sit up, then carefully to her feet. "Can you walk?"

"I can *run* if it'll get me out of here," she countered. "Though it may be a few moments before I can figure out which nerve works which leg."

"Fireman's carry it is."

Heaving her up across one shoulder, Agent Hessman then hurried as best he could back to the sliding door that Captain Beck was holding open and entered back into the control room. At the other door Ben was already getting it opened while Claire crowded in with the rest.

"Long hallway beyond," Ben reported. "From the looks of some of the hallway signs, we're in some sort of medical wing. This room is labeled as 'Op-Control C.'"

"First map of this place you see, grab it," Agent Hessman ordered. "We're winging it on the run here."

"Samantha, are you all right?" Claire asked as Ben flung the door wide and hurried out, holding it open for the rest.

"Upside down and light-headed," came the response, "but feeling a lot better. Just get me out of this chamber of futuristic horrors."

With Samantha carried over one shoulder, Agent Hessman led the charge down the medical hallway, the rest clustered around him, the other two men pulling out their respective Tasers, while Claire held on to her scarf as they ran.

"Always a chase," she remarked with a growing grin. "I think I'm going to like that part."

20

THE FAST TRIP DOWN

The hallway stretched on for a hundred feet left and right, all white-painted metal and smacking of that same overabundance of cleanliness that would define a hospital in nearly any age. A scattering of doors with similar palm-print security locks as their own adorned the hallway's length, each labeled with appropriate signage, their own door indeed labeled op-control c. To the right the hall came to an end at an extra-wide door labeled main operation theater, while the far-left end came to a T intersection with another hallway.

"Left," Agent Hessman immediately decided.

With Samantha carried over his shoulder, he immediately started into a hurried walk left, while Captain Beck took the lead with his Taser in hand, Ben and Claire covering their rear.

"I'd feel a lot better with Sue with us," Claire remarked as they hurried along. "She'd probably run on ahead, then just *assume* there'd be someone there and turn and shoot. Probably with some fancy cartwheel or split to avoid the other guy's guns."

"Unfortunately, Miss Hill," Agent Hessman called back, "Agent Harris is not with us on this one."

"But," Captain Beck remarked as he readied his weapon, "a good idea is still a good idea. Though I can't manage the cartwheel."

And so as they came up to the intersection, Captain Beck ran on ahead, then spun around facing left while firing off his Taser. Two wired darts flew out, impacting solidly into a target to deliver a full charge through the wires connecting them to the gun. Unfortunately, the target turned out to be a long and empty gurney left to one side of the hall, the darts having wrapped around the metal handles of one end of it.

Fortunately, an orderly stood there gripping the metal handles at the other end of the gurney, apparently just about to move the gurney away. Metal being rather conductive, the charge shot through the gurney and into the attending orderly, who spasmed once and then dropped.

"Well," Captain Beck noted as he pressed the retract button on his Taser, "not exactly what I had in mind, but—"

"Hospital Security. Hold it right there!"

Captain Beck froze, his hands rising slowly. The voice had come from the *right*-branching hall.

Hearing the new voice, Agent Hessman not only did *not* slow down from his fast walk with Samantha slung over his shoulder, but actually sped up while feeling her hands fishing around in his back pockets. He burst out into the middle of the T intersection, then turned to present his back to the presumed security guard. That meant, of course, that Samantha's draped upper body was facing the guard as she lifted her head with a brief smile and produced the gun she had just fished out of Agent Hessman's back pocket. Holding it in both hands, she took aim at the single guard she saw and fired.

It was another Taser, but fortunately, Samantha had a better shot lined up than Captain Beck. The pair of wired needles stuck not into his chest and the assumption of body armor, but in his face and into either cheek. The guard jerked, eyes rolling to the back of his head, foamed a little at the mouth, and then collapsed just as Ben and Claire emerged into the open.

"Now *that's* what I call teamwork," Claire said, beaming.

As Samantha pressed retract on the gun before putting it back in Agent Hessman's pocket, they all quickly appraised their current location. The left hallway was labeled b wing, the one they had just come from a wing, and the right branch reception.

"Reception it is," Agent Hessman said after a quick turn around to see his options. "Samantha, you may want to keep my gun handy since I find it difficult to carry you and shoot at the same time."

"Then you could always let me down," she said. "I think I can walk now. Not to mention that being upside down is turning out not to be the best thing for me right now."

As quickly as he could, and with a little help from Ben to steady her, Agent Hessman deposited Samantha back on her feet, whereupon she placed a hand to her forehead to steady herself before giving a slow nod to the others.

"Still a little out of it," Samantha reported, "but doing better."

"I'm afraid you'll have to shake it off on the run," Agent Hessman told her.

"I would think more of a hurried walk if we don't want to stand out," Claire put in.

"Miss Hill is right. The only ones after us are those Russians and the time police. Robert, hide the artillery."

As Captain Beck secured his Taser in his pocket, the group walked quickly down the right-hand hall, with Agent Hessman to Samantha's left and Ben to her right to support her. The hall ran just thirty feet before opening up into a wide vestibule. To their left was a large circular desk manned by receptionists and a couple of nurses, beyond which lay some sort of records room and nursing station; to their left, a couple of short rows of chairs and benches for prospective patients to wait. Straight ahead the wall was open to another mall-like view, this time of a slightly less gaudily lit medical court with offers for all manner of elective and emergency medical procedures.

Before anyone could wonder what to do, Claire immediately walked over to the reception desk.

"Excuse me, but we have someone who just came from having a procedure done and she's still a little groggy and we have a shuttle to catch. Do you have a pill or something to snap her out of it?"

The nurse-receptionist looked up, saw Claire's concerned smile and behind her the obviously distressed young lady being supported by the two men, and replied with a nod.

"Up too early against doctor's orders?" the receptionist asked.

"She's got some important work to get back to and has decided she's had enough fun in Space Vegas," Claire replied in a pleasant tone. "Personally, I'm amazed that we got her to stay *this* long. All business, you know."

"Got it," the nurse said with a grin. "I got some stuff that should fix her up."

Reaching around to a drawer behind the counter, the nurse quickly produced a pair of tiny pills wrapped in cellophane and handed them to Claire.

"Here. One now, then the other if she needs it, but nothing else after that. This stuff is probably illegal without a prescription most places planetside, but as the motto says, anything goes in Space Vegas."

"Oh, thank you. I don't know how I can repay you."

"Compliments of Space Vegas Medical Center. Anything to keep the gamblers awake and rolling."

Claire replied with a quick smile, then hurried back to the others and handed the packet to Samantha.

"This should fix you right up. One now, the other if that doesn't do it."

Samantha took the pills, carefully tore off the wrapper, and while she was taking one Agent Hessman offered a remark to Claire. "Miss Hill, anytime you wish to join my branch of government work I am sure that I can get you in."

Claire grinned in reply but said nothing more, just slipped back to Ben's other side as the group started moving forward. It was a short walk across the foyer to the edge of the mall court when Samantha spoke.

"Leaves a slight tingling in my mouth. Sort of like seltzer and . . ." She stopped, her eyes suddenly going wide.

"Samantha?" Agent Hessman asked. "Are you okay?"

She gave a slow nod in reply, then pushed away from the two men, standing now on her own.

"If you mean can I run for a mile or two without stopping, then yes," she finally replied. "What the *heck* was in that pill?"

"Enough to get us moving," Ben said. "Look."

Across the medical court, just coming out of a room advertising while-you-wait face-lifts, they saw another pair of temporal-police uniforms, one of them consulting a handheld instrument of some sort. The court was about one hundred fifty feet across, arranged in a circle, with two ways out: one about midway up the left-hand curve and another about midway up the right-hand curve. The pair of uniforms were closest to the left-hand exit. The court itself wasn't as crowded as the other places they had seen about, but crowded enough.

Agent Hessman immediately directed them around toward the right, making sure to keep close to Samantha.

"Fast walk, nothing suspicious, and everyone make sure to stay close to Samantha."

"Lou, I assure you, after that wake-up tablet, I can probably—"

"That's not it," he explained as they hurried along. "Those Russians had you here all this time, but there were no time cops tracking you down. This implies that they took you off the time cops' radar somehow, maybe with an implant of some sort."

"And if it *is* an implant," she said, "then why don't the rest of you reap the same benefit by sticking close to me. Got it."

They stayed as closely packed as they dared, everyone clustered around Samantha Weiss, as they walked around the clinic's perimeter and past another clinic specializing in "Zero-Gravity Radiometric Eye Surgery" and joined a crowd of people spilling out the left-hand exit. It was actually another wide hall, sweeping out in a slow curve that brought them along a passage lined with pop-up holographic ads for various entertainment venues.

Once out of sight of the medical court, it was Samantha who spoke up. "Can we run now? Yes, I want to run. Very far and very fast."

Agent Hessman looked at the tensely energetic expression on Samantha's face, then the wrapper with the second pill still in it and pried the wrapper loose from her grip and wadded it up into his pocket.

"No more of that for you," he decided. "And yes, I think it's time we picked up our pace."

"But where do we go?" Captain Beck asked. "They'll have the shuttle docks under watch by now."

"Option two," Agent Hessman replied. "Mr. Nezsmith mentioned a space elevator."

"He also mentioned it was experimental," Ben pointed out. "Not to mention that I didn't see a big long shaft stuck up in the underside of this place."

"Slender shaft, dark albedo—who says that you would have?" Agent Hessman countered. "Now let's hurry."

"Again, to where?" Captain Beck asked.

"Where else would you put a space elevator? This place had a bottom section. Let's head straight down."

Their hall expanded out into another multilevel promenade sporting clear elevators, walkways, deep drops, glittering casinos, one 3D holographic multiplex cinema, and a food court at one end with a large picture-window view of Earth, as well as lots of people. In the midst of the noise of flashing signs and audio entreaties to passersby, not to mention the passersby themselves, one sound stood out above it all in Agent Hessman's ears: the sound of running shoes quickly approaching from some distance behind them.

"Run!"

He led the way out into the middle of the open area, across a bridge spanning the central gap of the multistory drop, weaving through people without a glance back, and nearly across to the other side, where another sight stopped them: another pair of time cop uniforms on the other side of their bridge, waiting for them. A quick glance back confirmed that the running shoes had indeed been the pair from the medical court, now behind them and just coming onto the bridge.

"We have nowhere to go," Ben stated, "and the gravity around here's too strong to jump."

"We got one way," an urgent-looking Samantha said, sticking out a hand to Agent Hessman. "The second pill."

"Samantha, after seeing what one of those things can do to you, I do not think that—"

"Trust me. The pill."

With two sets of cops closing in through the march of pedestrians, it was Agent Hessman's time to trust in another's judgment. Quickly he took out the wrapper and squeezed the remaining pill into Samantha's hand. She took it without hesitating, then stood there for a few precious seconds.

The front pair of time cops were nearly thirty feet away when it hit her. Her entire body went tense, her eyes nearly bugging out as she grabbed the gun out of Agent Hessman's pocket and broke into a run, charging the pair of cops before them. Their response was predictable: they took out pistols similar to what they had seen the Russians use and fired. Two electrified bullets homed directly in on her, while at the same time Agent Hessman called out the charge for the rest.

The pair of temporal police saw a statuesque young brunette with bugged-out eyes running straight at them as the two projectiles hit her, but while both delivered their charges, they did not have the anticipated effect. Instead, they saw her aim and fire her own primitive gun while the others charged in behind her. One time cop found himself hit with a pair of needle-tipped electrified wires on the tip of his chin, while the other had a lithe, young body slam into him like a freight train.

Behind her, Agent Hessman came in with a fist to the face of the one still spasming from the Taser as Samantha tossed the gun away, Captain Beck following up Samantha's body slam on the other with a fist to the man's gut and a hard shove aside. Ben, meanwhile, picked up a pistol dropped by one of the cops, spun around, and fired it at the first cop he saw running up behind them. He didn't pause to see the result, just continued running on with the rest.

By this point the bystanders were screaming and ducking, trying to clear the way in whichever direction any of the combatants wanted to go. Once on the other side of the bridge, Agent Hessman managed to push ahead of Samantha, grab her by the hand, and lead them all through the screaming crowd toward the nearest glass elevator in a dead run, where he and Samantha shoved their way through to the head of the line, Claire apologizing to one elderly man along the way.

The elevator doors closed with Captain Beck punching the lowest-numbered button that he could find on the panel. As the car shot down to the sight of one frustrated team of cops helping the other team back up to their feet, Ben shot a questioning look to Samantha, who briefly explained her action.

"I just figured that the way that first pill hit me, it must be a derivative of PCP. People high on that stuff are just about impervious to pain."

"And if it was designed to quickly revive someone," Agent Hessman said, picking up her train of thought, "then a double dose just might provide some protection against those electrified bullets of theirs. Good call. But I worry about possible overdose effects."

"Getting hit twice by those charged bullets seems to have taken the edge off," she replied. "But what now? How do we find our way off this thing?"

"No buttons labeled 'Space Elevator,'" Captain Beck reported, "but I did find a card reader."

At the bottom of the panel of buttons was indeed a slot that looked perfect for something about the size of a credit card. Ben was closest and stepped over, saw the size of the slot, and grinned. Taking out the transport card that Jeffery Nezsmith had given him, he slid it in and spoke out loud: "We want to go to the space elevator. Please take us there and ready a ride down."

A light on the panel blinked, the panel of buttons disappearing to be replaced by a display that read "Space Elevator Express," and his card popped back out as the elevator sped on a bit faster.

"As automated and interlinked as everything around here is . . . ," Ben said with a shrug.

"Another good call," Agent Hessman stated.

The elevator shot them down through level after level, directly past a couple more open courts, then a long trip past nothing but windowed views of space as they passed into the lower section and on through a dozen more levels before coming to a smooth stop. The elevator doors, however, did not open.

"They trapped us," Claire said with a worried look.

But then the elevator began moving again, only this time *sideways*. To Claire's confused look, Agent Hessman offered his own opinion.

"The odds of us picking an elevator that happened to be the one to go directly to the space elevator were astronomical. It figures they would have a system like this set up."

"It does say 'Express,'" Ben stated. "I guess they really meant it."

When the elevator finally opened, it was to a relatively small reception area. In fact, it had just the one elevator, two hallway doors out, and directly across from them a set of heavy-looking double doors. The only people there were one man dressed prim and proper in his suit and tie and a less formal-looking technician at a control stand to one side of the double doors.

"Welcome to Space Vegas' Elevator to the Stars," the man said. "Be careful as you walk: we're close to weightless around here. Just step purposefully and don't shuffle, and the floor's static grid will hold you down. Now, do you all have your transport cards?"

They stepped carefully out, walking as the man had instructed and finding that, while they could still feel that weightless sensation in the pits of their stomachs, their feet nonetheless grabbed on to the floor as if magnetized—except there was nothing about their footwear to be magnetically drawn.

Claire's long hair was floating around as if underwater, yet the rest of her was not. The mixed sensation earned a wide-mouthed, voiceless exclamation from her as they each produced a transport card. All save Samantha, who had none, but as the man went around with his hand scanner to quickly scan the cards, Agent Hessman spoke up for her.

"Put her on my card, or divide it up among them all if you have to."

"It looks like there should be enough left on the account," the man said, glancing at his reader. Then, after confirming the fact, he broke out into a smile. "I hope you enjoyed your stay at Space Vegas. You have chosen a magnificent way to end your trip, as I assure you there is nothing like what you are about to experience."

The technician pressed something on his control board and the double doors before them opened, followed by another inner set of similar doors. Agent Hessman led the way across while the man continued going on about their impending ride and various safety procedures, most of which they all ignored in their urgency to be away.

"The floor of the elevator car also has a grid floor just like this one to hold you down, but just remember about the straps and handholds should things get a little too intense, and have a safe and enjoyable trip down."

They piled into the chamber, which looked like a normal elevator car save that it was surrounded by a lot of extra armored metal inside and out, and had padded walls, and a single window behind them to catch the view from space. Claire wasn't the only one fascinated by the view as the heavy doors closed behind them. Outside was a dark well of infinity; far below them a gigantic blue marble.

"Drop in five, four, three . . ."

As the mechanical voice rang out, a counter appeared in the air before the inner door. At "two" everyone grabbed on to the available handrails and straps and braced themselves.

". . . one. Drop."

It felt like the world fell away through the pits of their stomachs. A jerk at first, then confusion as their weightless environment fought against the momentum of their downward flight. A glance out through the window showed no movement of the distant stars, though it did seem as if that large blue marble was very gradually increasing in size.

"I feel weird!" Claire screamed out. "I'm not sure I like this part of the trip."

"It should feel better at about the midway point, once we start feeling Earth's gravity," Samantha called back. "We're probably already going faster than the speed of sound."

"Hopefully, this thing's got good brakes," Captain Beck remarked. "But what happens once this thing drops us off wherever it's going?"

"We're not waiting that long," Agent Hessman announced. "If it was me, I'd just have a very large security detail waiting for us at the bottom."

"Then how . . . ," Claire began.

"Beacons out everyone," Agent Hessman ordered. "The instant we're in range, activate them!"

Down through infinity they fell, the view somewhere between thrilling and stomach churning. Beacons were taken out and constantly checked, everyone waiting for the red warning light to stop flashing and inform them they were back in range. Once they passed through the upper atmosphere, everyone began desperately thumbing buttons as the view outside expanded to show them now dropping down in a fall their minds *could* grasp as lands far below came into view. Claire was shaking and holding on to her rail with a death grip, but through it all, Ben's arm lent a reassuring hug around her waist.

"It's a pity I already asked you to marry me," he said, "because this would have been the *perfect* place to pop the question."

"You could ask me again," she said with a more relaxed smile. "I might even give you the same answer."

Suddenly red lights turned green on their beacons, and Agent Hessman quickly wrapped an arm around Samantha and drew her in tight.

When the space elevator came to a gentle stop on Earth, the dozen armed time cops waiting in the reception area before the landing station doors saw them finally open to reveal the inside of the elevator car. It was completely empty.

21

BACK IN THE PRESENT

The lids on all the pods popped open as the large propeller-like arms slowed to a stop. The team members lay in their pods just as they had been before, but now a previously empty extra pod produced a new passenger. While the rest saw the helping hands of technicians assisting them out of their pods, Samantha Weiss saw the face of her uncle ready to assault her with a bear hug the second the technician tending her stepped away.

"Samantha! You're safe!"

He was dressed in the same clothes he'd had on when the team had left, but now looking as if he had been sleeping in them, lines earned from long hours of worrying tracing deeply through his features.

"Uncle!"

Agent Harris was there as well, still in her hospital gown and slippers, greeting Claire and Ben with a grin and sporting a cane.

"So, what'd I miss?"

"*Wow!*" Claire remarked as they both got to their feet. "Now *that* was a ride."

"I think my stomach's still back up in orbit," Captain Beck remarked as he climbed out of his pod. "Though on the plus side, I don't think I have to worry about my motion sickness anymore."

"And the shuttle ride up, all the fantastic things we saw, those holographic park statues," Claire excitedly listed off. "I can hardly wait to write my next article!"

"One which a certain Jeffery Nezsmith will apparently not get to read before we encounter him," Ben added. Then to Agent Harris: "We have quite the story to tell."

"Well, the general wants a briefing as soon as everyone's able," she replied. "Now, about this wedding I seem to remember someone mentioning when I was regaining consciousness. Because I've been having cane races with Dr. Weiss trying to get back into shape for the thing."

Claire grinned. "Sue, we all really missed having you along."

As Claire was giving Agent Harris a heartfelt hug, a tearful Dr. Sam Weiss was just pulling back from his niece to look her over.

"I was worried every second you were gone, my dear."

"You can thank Lou here that I'm back at all. How long was I gone? Or for that matter, *when* is it anyway?"

"Friday, about ten minutes to three in the morning."

"That means . . . tomorrow's Saturday."

Samantha raised her right hand to the side of her head, massaging gently while Agent Hessman came up beside her, though refraining from anything but a respectful distance in the presence of watching official eyes.

"Sam, my dear, what is it?" Dr. Weiss asked.

"I . . . Nothing. Just a little tired, I guess."

"After all you've been through," Agent Hessman said, "including coming down off those pills, you just need some rest. I'll escort you to your room."

"Of course," Dr. Weiss said with a sigh of relief. "But be sure to fill me in on everything later."

"Sure . . . Of course, Uncle."

But as Agent Hessman started leading her away, she suddenly stopped short as a thought popped into her head.

"Of course. Tomorrow's Saturday. I have a think tank at Caltech to attend tomorrow. Lou, do you think that you could arrange for a flight?"

"I can arrange for some bed time. You don't look like you're ready to go anywhere."

"Please? This is very important."

He looked her in the eye and saw the fatigue written therein but also the need and concern behind it.

"Devotion to duty. I can understand that. Okay. I can get a flight straight from this base, but only if you stop by the mess hall to grab something to eat and some vitamins or something."

"I can pick up something from the infirmary and eat on the plane. Thank you, Lou."

Dr. Weiss watched as Agent Hessman escorted his niece away, a frown crossing his features as he saw the preoccupied look on Samantha's face.

* * *

It was later in one of the conference rooms. Dr. Weiss was sitting alone thinking to himself when Agent Harris walked in.

"Sam, you up for another cane race? I'll even spot you five feet."

"What? Er . . . no. Not right now."

Agent Harris paused for a more careful look at Dr. Weiss, particularly at the way he was steepling his fingers and the worried look on his face.

"Okay, something's wrong," she stated. "What is it?"

"What?" he said, looking up. "Oh, nothing really. Just a little paranoid probably."

He tried replying with a smile, but Agent Harris maintained her fixed glare.

"Okay," he confessed, "so there's just something a little off about Samantha."

That's when Agent Hessman walked in, his attention immediately fixed on the exchange.

"Off how?" Agent Harris asked.

"Well, she's . . . usually more vivacious. I realize how much she must have been through, but I've seen her pull an all-nighter studying and still have enough left in her for a smile and a joke. I didn't see that tonight. She seemed . . . unusually preoccupied. Unfocused."

"She might still be recovering," Agent Hessman told them. "We found her strapped to an operating table, being prepped for some procedure."

"Yes," Dr. Weiss said with a tired nod, "I suppose that could be it."

"And she did still have enough left in her to hop on that plane a little bit ago," Agent Hessman added.

Agent Harris, however, was still maintaining her focused glare, only now she directed it at Agent Hessman as she turned around to face him.

"A procedure? Lou . . . what makes you think that they didn't already do to her whatever they were going to do? How do you know they didn't *want* you to take her when you did?"

Both Agent Hessman and Dr. Weiss were silent for a moment as the import of her question sank in. Then it was Agent Hessman's turn to ask a question.

"Sam, this think tank of Samantha's—do you know what it's about and who's in it?"

"Well, near as I can get," came the reply, "they consider any number of subjects, though I don't know what it is currently. As far as who's on it, there's . . . let's see, a Dr. Greg Stevens, Dr. Amanda Beckett, a corporate suit from one of the big biomedical companies, Dr. Dillon Marshal, and I think—"

"Wait! Did you say *Dillon Marshal?*"

"Why yes. Young kid, got some ideas about—"

"A plastic-eating bug that gets out of control," Agent Hessman said quietly, cutting in.

"A what?" Agent Harris asked.

"I think Sam did mention something about Dr. Marshal coming up with a pollution solution," Dr. Weiss remarked, "but I don't think that—"

"It's the Manchurian candidate," Agent Hessman muttered.

He nearly leaped over to grab Dr. Weiss, pulling him to his feet and quickly telling him, "We've got a plane to catch. I'll explain on the way." As Dr. Weiss stood looking confused, Agent Hessman planted a quick kiss on Agent Harris's cheek on his way toward the door.

"Sue, how I've missed that lovely paranoia of yours."

He hurried out into the hall, Dr. Weiss in a fast hobble behind him, and tapped a finger to the com device in his right ear.

"This is Hessman. I need a military jet ready to fly by the time I get up to the surface. Urgent! And notify Chief Duke and Professor Stein. Samantha Weiss is in trouble."

Hearing that was enough to make Dr. Weiss dare breaking into a run to keep up with Agent Hessman.

22

CALTECH TRAGEDY

It was nearly nine in the morning that Saturday by the time they found themselves racing across the Caltech campus. The jet had been prepped by the time Agent Hessman was able to drag Dr. Weiss along with him, with Chief Duke already there waiting for him and Ben and Claire running up to join them. After that it was a ride in the fastest jet available, though Claire seemed amazingly relaxed through the entire trip. Something about "After flying up into space, then falling back down to Earth, this seems kinda slow and mundane."

As they all sat in the large jet's cargo section on the flight over, with the radio linked up to General Karlson back at the base, Agent Hessman explained his suspicions to both the general and those with him.

"After what Agent Harris suggested, I realized there's only one reason they would have let Samantha go. Somehow they've mentally programmed her to carry out a mission back in our time. That's the only way they've found to really change their past—to get *us* to do it for them."

"But why Samantha?" a worried Dr. Weiss asked.

"Because of who's a member of this think tank and the reason why the Russians are so interested in her—Dillon Marshal."

"Uh-oh," Ben remarked with a frown. "That explains the Russians, alright."

"Not to me it doesn't," Dr. Weiss said with a shake of his head.

"Or to me," came General Karlson's voice from the radio speaker overhead.

"Dillon Marshal creates a bug that eats all the waste plastic in the oceans," Agent Hessman explained, "only it gets out of control, with Russia in particular getting the worst of it. They'll do anything to prevent that from having happened. I figured that seeing her uncle might help, and Miss Hill seems to have a way with people, but once we hit the ground . . ."

"There will be a military escort waiting for you when you hit the ground. Take it anywhere you need and save Miss Weiss."

The remainder of their trip mainly consisted of Dr. Weiss expressing his worries, while Claire couldn't help but see the overly stern expression on Agent Hessman's face and wonder what concerns lay behind it. Their ride later from the airport involved a lot of screaming sirens, from the landing strip straight into the city of Pasadena, followed by Agent Hessman leading the charge across the Caltech campus as he called back to Dr. Weiss hobbling along behind him.

"Do you have any idea where this think tank meets?"

"Uh . . . Dabney Hall, I think. Straight ahead."

To their left was a long reflection pool; around it and before them, grassy landscaping and cement walkways on all sides, the whole like a glade in a forest of squat one- and two-story structures given over to intellectual pursuits. The far-left end of the pool marked entry into a distinctive tall white-and-gray building stabbing like a finger up to the sky. To their right were some gardens and small ponds, but directly ahead of them, through a series of arches decorating one of the walkways, was an old two-story building that, from its architecture, could have either been one of the original campus school buildings or an aging mausoleum.

Agent Hessman bolted straight across the gardened quad, pushing past a couple of students in the way, the only one keeping up with him being Chief Duke. Chief Duke leaped ahead of him as they came to the building, taking the four slight steps up in a single bound and nearly ripping the double doors open before Agent Hessman, who then charged in.

A hallway stretched on before them. The left side sported a scattered line of doors, each labeled with someone's name. To their immediate right a short flight of stairs curved downward, past which only a single set of doors farther on marked the expanse of the remaining length of hall.

Agent Hessman went straight for the singular set of doors on the right.

Ben and Claire came in with Dr. Weiss just in time to see Agent Hessman run through the doors to the room beyond.

"Go on ahead," Dr. Weiss told them. "And when you see Samantha . . ."

"Don't worry, we'll save her," Ben replied.

The room was an auditorium of sorts, but one with a wall of glass doors along the left side opening out onto a patio, and a fireplace at the far end. A long table was set up in the middle, several figures already seated around it with their laptops. A large flat-screen monitor rigged up on its own small stand before the middle of the side facing the fireplace displayed the apparent object of their discussion.

"Excuse me," one of the people there said, "but this is a private meeting. You can't just . . ."

Agent Hessman had his picture ID out in a flash as he quickly approached.

"Special Agent Lou Hessman. We're looking for Dr. Samantha Weiss."

"She hasn't arrived yet," another answered, "though she's a little overdue. Now what is . . . ?"

"I want you all to vacate this building immediately," Agent Hessman ordered. "Which one of you is Dillon Marshal?"

One scruffy-looking young man with light-brown hair stood up uncertainly, but before he or anyone else could speak, Agent Hessman was already giving out another command while Chief Duke went about bodily yanking protesting people out of their seats and shoving them in the direction of the patio doors.

Dillon Marshal - Inventor Plastic Eating Bug

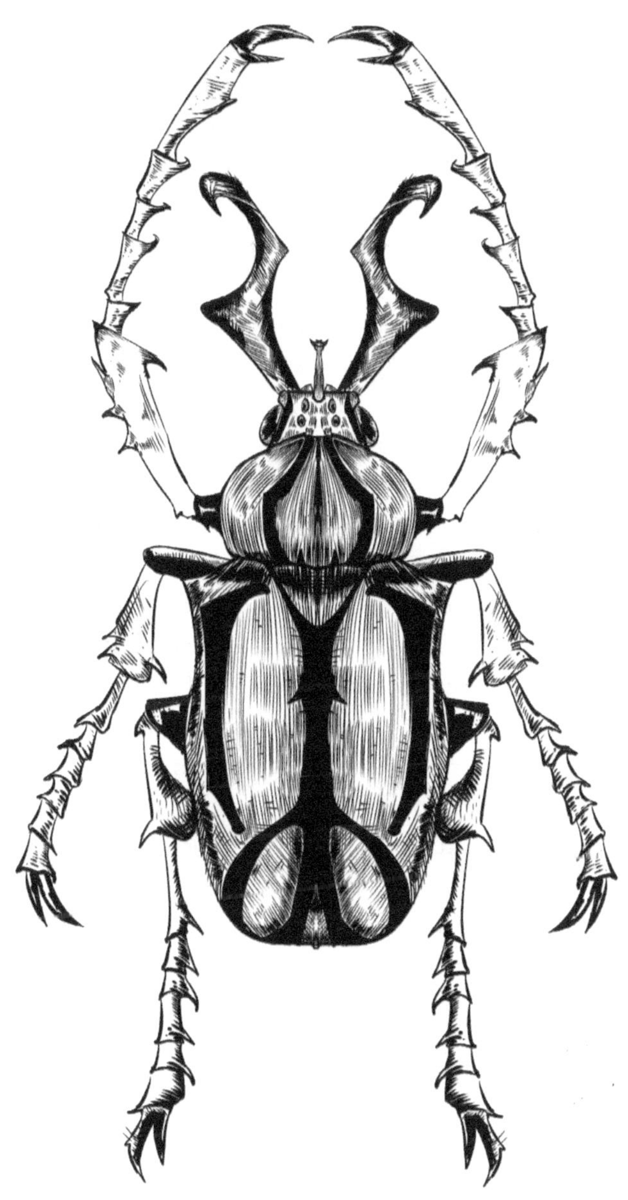

Plastic Eating Bug

"You especially," he ordered the young man, "just run until you see the street or a bomb shelter."

A quick visual survey of the room showed him nothing, so it was back out the door he went, where he bumped into Ben and Claire on their way in, with Dr. Weiss a few paces behind them.

"She's not here. But this *has* to be— Sam, what's directly below this room?"

"Basement," he answered, pointing with his cane. "Those stairs over there."

"Has to be it, then. Chief Duke with me. Ben, if you and Claire have to, *lift* Sam down those stairs," Agent Hessman said, pushing past them. "I suspect he's going to be needed. I'm hoping the face of a loved one will snap her out of it."

"If I have to grow wings and fly," Dr. Weiss swore, "I will. That's my *niece!*"

Agent Hessman ran down the short flight they had seen coming in, a turn and down a similar flight, with Chief Duke right alongside. The stairs led them down into a short corridor ending at an open pair of doors beyond which was another large room. This one, though, was crowded with various storage shelves, crates, and equipment, at the center and off to the far right of which they could see a light and hear the sounds of something being moved across the floor.

Agent Hessman put a finger to his lips for Chief Duke, then, as Ben and Claire appeared at the top of the second flight of stairs, motioned them down and pointed in the direction of the sounds. Carefully he crept around a turn in the storage shelves and finally into view of the lit section. Several yards away he saw a table, on top of which rested an assemblage of wires and electronics, all based around a pair of foot-high ceramic cylinders wired to one another at the top.

Putting the final touches on the contraption was Samantha. Her gaze was distant and fixed as she made the last few connections, just staring off into space as she muttered one phrase over and over again like a mantra.

"To save the future. To save the future. To save the future."

Agent Hessman motioned Chief Duke into hiding behind the storage shelves while he straightened up and stepped into view, gently calling out, "Samantha. It's Lou."

She paused only briefly to look up and fix Lou with a gaze that looked like a stranger's. "I've got to save the future," she blandly stated.

"Samantha, listen. Those Russians from the future did something to mess with your head. You've got to fight it."

"I've got to save the future."

"Samantha, you've got to hear me. You recognize me, right? I'm Lou Hessman. We met at Los Alamos when your conference got crashed. Remember?"

"Hess-man," she slowly stated.

"Yes. Those Russians brainwashed you. You can't . . ."

"To save the future," she repeated, at which point she went back to her work.

"Okay, try this. I've already been upstairs and evacuated the room. Dillon Marshal is safe. Your mission is scrubbed. Do you hear me? Your target is no longer available."

"Sam!"

Hobbling in behind Agent Hessman came Dr. Weiss. He pushed away from Ben and Claire and set a gradual pace for his niece.

"This isn't you, Sam. You don't kill people; you won't even step on a bug."

For a moment her gaze flickered, her face filled with a look of recognition. "Uncle Sam?"

"Yes, dear, it's me," Dr. Weiss tearfully replied. "Now just stop what you're doing and come to me."

Meanwhile, Agent Hessman had slipped into the shadows, leaving the more familiar face of Dr. Weiss to awaken Samantha's mind.

"I . . . can't. I've got to save— Uncle, I think . . . I think something's wrong."

"I'm here for you, Sam. Your uncle."

Two more slow steps, and for a second it looked as if his niece might break, but suddenly her face went blank and her head snapped up with a stern glare at her uncle.

"Primary target aborted. Secondary target acquired."

At least one person there didn't wait for Samantha to finish the motion of bringing her right hand up, didn't wait to see the gun she now held. As Dr. Weiss gasped at the sight of his own niece about to gun him down, a large body caught him in the side with a flying tackle just as the trigger was pulled back, while somewhere behind them Ben and Claire both hit the ground. To the sharp echo of the pistol sounding off, Chief Duke tackled Dr. Weiss to the ground, the bullet missing the large Navy SEAL by inches.

The gun had barely finished firing when another body came flying out of the shadows, but this one toward Samantha. It was Agent Hessman. He tackled her away from the table, knocking the gun out of her hand as he pinned her to the ground.

"No," Samantha said as she struggled. "I've got to complete the mission. I've got to . . ."

She suddenly stopped struggling, her face clearing and eyes blinking.

"Lou?"

Once Agent Hessman had made his tackle, Chief Duke released Dr. Weiss and picked him up to his feet as Ben and Claire got up as well to join him in surrounding the prone young woman in a small sea of concerned faces. Samantha saw first Agent Hessman and then her uncle hobbling up behind him.

"Uncle . . . Sam," she said. "I . . . I'm sorry."

"It's okay, Sam," Dr. Weiss replied, tears in his eyes. "It wasn't you."

"Samantha," Agent Hessman began, "we've got to keep you bound until we can figure out how to fix you up, but we *will* find a way."

"I know, but I . . . I'm sorry. My God, I was about to shoot my own uncle! And, Lou . . ."

For a moment Samantha's eyes held a look for Lou that Ben recognized as the same way that Claire looked at him. Then Samantha's face went blank, her gaze fixed, and her body began convulsing.

"Sam!"

Chief Duke held Dr. Weiss back before he could do anything foolish, while Ben held on to Claire.

"No," Lou stated, now shaking Samantha by the shoulders. "Stop. Ben, get a call out to our escort for an emergency evac. Samantha, come back to me!"

Chief Duke produced a palm-sized radio unit and tossed it to Ben to make the call, while a broken Dr. Weiss dropped to his knees. This left Claire to simply stare as Lou tried to control Samantha's convulsions in a tight hug, and perhaps she was the only one to see the expression on his face and the single tear that rolled down his cheek while Samantha's eyes rolled back in her head.

23

A TEAR AND A SMILE

It was Sunday morning back at the base in New Mexico, where an anxious little crowd waited outside a private ward of the infirmary. Samantha lay inside on a bed while a doctor and two nurses tended her. She was hooked up to several tubes and wires and was surrounded by a short wall of medical equipment. The room had one wall with a mirror covering its entire length, the other side of the two-way mirror being the observation room from which the crowd now watched.

Dr. Weiss was there, not using his cane for much more than worriedly tapping with as he watched the procedures, while Lou looked on like a lovelorn puppy, trying his best to school his features. Ben and Claire were there, too, as were Agent Harris, Captain Beck, and, most notably, General Karlson as they received a report from the head doctor and infirmary administrator.

"Whatever it was they did to program her, it had a fail-safe," the doctor was saying. "Our best guess is that if either of her missions were to fail, she would suffer a seizure. She's alive, but . . ."

He paused to look at Dr. Weiss and Agent Hessman, the latter straightening up before turning his usual stern face back.

"Continue, Doctor," he said. "What is the full prognosis?"

Dr. Weiss, too, turned to regard the doctor, though he had no problem displaying his worry clearly for all to read.

"As it stands she is all but brain-dead, and in a very deep coma. We have her on full life-support, but we really don't know if she'll ever pull out. Whatever they've done, it's on a level of medicine and the brain that we have yet to reach. Our best guess is that she's in there somewhere, but . . ." He ended with a shrug, to which the general gave a nod.

"I see," General Karlson said. "We'll keep up the care for as long as it takes. The second she walked onto this base she was one of our family, and I never give up on family. Doctor, I expect regular updates on her condition. The least little improvement . . ."

"And I will notify you immediately, of course," the doctor replied.

"Dr. Weiss," the general said, turning to Sam, "what did you want me to tell her parents?"

"I'll tell them myself," he replied. "Avoiding all the classified stuff, of course. She was attacked by some terrorists and now lies in a coma. That's the basic truth of it, after all."

"I'll leave it to you then," the general stated. "Doctor, you can get back to your charges."

The doctor left with a nod, leaving the general and the team to regard their fallen friend through the two-way mirror as her personal doctor and nurses tended to her.

"Since the subject seems to be before us," General Karlson remarked, "and with respect to everyone's feelings, I want to know what we can do to prevent any further interference from the future. I don't care *how* bad it is in the future, they have no right to ambush us like this. If they want to change the future, then they could have the courtesy to *tell* us what it is that's about to go wrong and let *us* judge what should be done next."

"With respect, General," Dr. Weiss said with a sniff, "and with all due respect to my own loss, I'm not only unsure if we *can* change the future but if we should even *try*."

"Explain."

With a last look back at his niece so still on the hospital bed, he faced the others with his explanation.

"Those Russians from the future have already changed *their* present by putting my niece into a coma. Not even they can foretell what repercussions that may have, what discoveries she might have otherwise made that they relied upon. Or what her discoveries might have inspired others to achieve. It's a domino effect, a chain reaction that might have already destroyed some segment of the future that they were trying to hold on to."

"Sam's right," Ben put in. "They may have the more advanced tech, but they lack the wisdom. To change whatever they've been suffering through, those future Russians acted in panic, and that's never a good decision-making policy. And I would like to point out that there may be other things they may have inadvertently changed with their actions."

"For instance?" the general prompted.

"Well, for instance: Did that plastic-eating bug get out of control because of some input of Samantha's," Ben replied, "or does it now get out of control because she's not there with her think-tank group to point out its flaws? For all we know, they might have cursed themselves to their own undesirable future. History is riddled with self-fulfilling prophecies."

"In which case, they may find themselves even more desperate and make yet another journey back into our time," Captain Beck pointed out. "Or maybe the results of their actions have now made a different group desperate enough to come back."

"It gives me a headache just thinking about it, but you all have a point," the general agreed. "Recommendations?"

Dr. Weiss sniffed once more, wiped the tears from his face with his free hand, and then faced up to the general with what he hoped was more his usual self. "I can start work on improving the temporal scanners. With some tweaking I should be able to get them to detect an incoming temporal displacement wave before it actually touches down. That would give us some time to get a team on the spot to greet our intruders before they can do any harm."

"Then get to it," the general snapped.

"Immediately, sir."

A last look at his sleeping niece, a quick nod to the general, and a glance to his fellow team members, and Dr. Weiss headed for the door. Before he left, however, Agent Hessman called to him.

"Wait . . . Sam. Is there any chance that we can just go back and do something to save Samantha? Maybe even before she's kidnapped."

Dr. Weiss sighed. "I'm afraid not. And she would be the first to agree with me. We would only risk messing up something else the way those Russians have done, and *they* were supposedly more skilled at this sort of thing than we are."

"Got it," Agent Hessman replied in a subdued tone. "I had to ask."

Dr. Weiss left without another word said, at which point the general addressed the rest.

"And if ever anyone has some other recommendations," he said, "no matter how ridiculous sounding, I want to hear them. Even you, Miss Hill."

"Me? But I don't know anything about this sort of stuff."

"You have a proven ability at thinking on your feet and reading people that some would find envious, and on recommendation of certain others you are hereby a permanent member of this team."

"Recommendations? But who would recommend me for something *this* important?"

"Well"—beside her Ben shrugged—"I might have had a word with General Karlson during a recent debriefing."

"You?" Captain Beck put in. "I thought it was *my* recommendation."

"I heard the highlights and may have made a suggestion to the general," Agent Harris added.

"It looks like it was unanimous," Agent Hessman remarked. "Since I'm guessing that Sam had a word or two with the general as well—not to mention myself."

"Your official designation," the general continued with a slight grin, "will be team reporter and humanities advisor. Assuming you want the job, of course."

Claire's answer was to hug herself close to Ben's side and return the general's grin with a more open smile.

"I thought I'd left my entire family back in 1919. I guess I was wrong."

"It comes with a paycheck, of course," the general continued. "But I'm afraid that very few people will be reading your reports, since they'll be classified for quite a while to come."

"Oh, I expected that. In fact, I knew it before you mentioned it. But if you don't mind, could my *unofficial* title be something a little different?"

"Such as?"

She paused for a moment, directing her smile now to Ben at her side, who replied for her.

"She means 'Claire Hill . . . cross-temporal reporter.'"

The general chuckled but nodded his agreement, then finally focused on Agent Hessman with a more serious look.

"Lou, are you going to be okay? It seems as half the base noticed your affection for Miss Weiss."

Lou turned for a last look at an unconscious Samantha Weiss, gave one last sniff, and straightened. Gone were the sorrow, the lovelorn features, and any tears he might have shed; replaced with the stern, calculating look that all there had come to know him by.

"I will be fine, General. I was merely reminded of a basic rule of my profession."

"And what is that?" the general asked.

"That for what it is that I do . . . I cannot afford attachments. This won't happen again, and I would be most appreciative if no one else says anything more of this."

He said that last with a look particularly at Claire, who replied only with a slow nod and a single tear leaking from the edge of one eye.

"Understood," the general replied.

All eyes turned for a last look at Samantha Weiss, their heads hanging in collective memoriam. Some tears were shed, but never again by Agent Hessman. For that, Claire shed two tears: one for herself and one for the tears that she knew Lou dare not give.

Claire holding Holographic Photo

* * *

Later that evening, Claire was in her room on the base arranging things to her liking and unpacking one particular artifact: a slender electronic card the size of an old Polaroid photograph. As she held it out on her hand a picture sprang up in full three-dimensional glory of her and a young man grinning before a background of some futuristic airport. She sighed to see the picture, then, after another glance around, decided on one corner of a bookshelf as its final home.

"Now what on earth is *that*?"

Claire spun around to see Agent Harris standing in the doorway, leaning on her cane.

"My first memento," she replied. "Apparently of many. A hundred years from now Jeffery Nezsmith will be giving me this."

She held it up for Agent Harris to better see, then settled it into its place before crossing the room to join her friend.

"Though I suppose after Ben and I are married we'll both just have to find a bigger room to move into."

"Why not move in together now? You've already slept together, right?"

"Sue, please," Claire replied with mock shock. "I do have *some* sensibilities from my birth century, you know . . . Which I guess is the one memento that I'll always have of my time: myself."

"I suppose that's true enough," Agent Harris admitted with a slight grin.

"But I'm just glad to see you on your feet again. How much longer until you no longer need the cane?"

"Doc says about a week. Then I'm back on active duty."

"That'll be great, because that other guy they had filling in for you just didn't cut it. Agent Stevens? You could have replaced him with a robot . . . Uh, he really *isn't* a robot or something, right? Because I never know with this time period."

"No, he's human . . . technically. Anyway, I just came to tell you that I have an update from General Karlson."

"Something serious?"

"Depends on who you are. He just got word from the Joint Chiefs. They've agreed to expand the time travel program so as to include more international cooperation. The argument goes that things would benefit from the increased variety of expertise, not to mention that something like this is too dangerous for any single nation to possess."

"I guess that means we could have an Italian as the next bodyguard of the day."

"The next *what*?"

To Sue's perplexed look, Claire broke out into a wide smile.

"Something Jeffery mentioned. Apparently Lieutenant Phelps was reassigned. But continue; it sounds like there's more."

"There is . . . After this latest incident, the Joint Chiefs have agreed that both the past *and* the future must be protected. In fact, someone's bandying about the term 'temporal guardians,' though that sounds a bit much to me."

"Pretentious," Claire agreed. "Maybe something more like 'time cops' or 'temporal police.'"

It would be a while before Agent Harris would know why Claire started giggling after saying that.

"I can see that I'll be needing a more in-depth reading of that report you'll be typing up to get caught up on all the in-jokes."

"Excuse me," Claire objected, "but I'm a reporter, which makes it an *article*. And yes, you have a little bit of catching up to do."

"I look forward to it."

As Agent Harris was mulling over Claire's amusement, Ben approached from the hallway outside, coming up to stand beside Sue with a question for his betrothed.

"Have you asked her yet?"

To Sue's questioning look, Claire started to explain.

"I mentioned something about it before we left for the mission, but now that you're more fully up and awake I wanted to make it official. You see, Ben and I have finally set a date."

"Congratulations," Sue replied. "I'm sure it'll be the biggest wedding that no one outside this base will ever have the clearance to know about."

"And I would be honored if . . . Well, would you be my maid of honor?"

Sue replied with a smile whose width nearly seemed out of place on her face, and a slight nod.

"You *do* remember how I promised to dropkick anyone else you would have asked? I may have just been cming out of a coma at the time, but I remember you asking the first time, and it will be *my* honor."

"Great," Claire replied with a sense of relief. "After all, I wouldn't want to mess up the future, now would I?"

She said this with a wink to Ben and nothing else explained. Not that Sue needed any explanations in that moment; she just hobbled over to Claire and gave her a big hug . . . and then pulled in Ben along with her.